Tied Him To The Tropes

S.L. Simmons

This book is a work of fiction. Although, at times inspired by real life as well as quotes, any names of characters, businesses or places, events or incidents are fictitious. No identification with actual persons, living or dead, products, or actual brand, is intended or should be inferred.

No part of this publication may be reproduced, distributed, or transmitted in any form or by any means, including photocopying, recording, or other electronic or mechanical methods, without the prior written permission of the author, except as permitted by U.S. copyright law. For permission requests, contact the publisher.

K.J. Arias has been used in producing this book.

Book cover: S.L. Shemaitis

First edition: September 2025

www.slshemaitisworldsmith.com

For those that like a little plot with their smut,
know that biketok is just masktok with the zoomies,
and dream of their own helmeted hero to worship.

Tied Him To The Tropes by Ruby Darkrose (2025) is my inspiration for this book and due to copyrighting laws, I cannot place the lyrics that go with each chapter as I would have liked but did try to name the chapters so that you, the reader, know which lines went with that chapter.

Listen on YouTube HERE
And Spotify HERE

Tied Him To The Tropes by Ruby Darkrose

For Content & Trigger Warnings

and

Genre/Trope Listing

visit

www.slsimmonswordsmith.com

Contents

Contents

In no way is this book anything but pure fiction.
Do not use it or any part of any fictional work
as a blueprint for life.

Consent is *not* optional.
Personal space is just that.

CHAPTER THREE

Ruby

Sunlight filling the front windows as the clouds parted for a millisecond from today's rainy weather brought my attention from the coffee stain I was scrubbing. Lunch was over and we would be slow now until the after dinner rush of friends meeting before finding something fun to do and corporate types needing a caffeine fix to burn the midnight oil. Nectar of the gods filled the air, underlined with ink and warm parchment.

Sitting right on the edge of the sidewalk, just under the overhang in case more rain chose to pour down, was the sleekest, blackest bike I had ever laid eyes on. How I had missed its arrival just showed how in my head I had become. Dragging my eyes to the rider leaning against the seat, I took in his head to toe ensemble that matched the bike. Pads didn't need to enhance what was a leanly muscled frame, filling out the leather fitting him like a second skin.

Visor open, gloves on the seat next to him, he tapped away on his phone, thumbs flying. Looking behind at the steaming parking lot that was giving him an epic background effect, then up at the sky rapidly turning from hammered steel to robin's egg blue, he laid his phone down with his gloves, reaching for that tab at his throat.

Glancing around, I made sure Brittany wasn't in the vicinity to catch me drooling before turning back to the show that was now filling what would have been a boring afternoon with a much needed feature film I was going to file into my rub hub. Lord knows I needed it.

Keeping my ears open for the approach of those damn high heels the cashier from the book store side of the café I worked in thought appropriate to wear, I followed the slow descent of that zipper. Tanned skin with swirls of ink appeared. Calling in every favor I could bribe any deity with, I prayed he was shirtless under that leather.

Being far from any form of religious had me being left in the lurch as under the upper portion of his one piece suit was not bare skin. It was the second best thing. A thin under tank in cherry red molded to that lean body that was hinted at by the leather wrapping him like a well worn glove.

Sleeves tied around his waist, phone back in his hand, helmet still on, he wiped his equally black boots before opening the door on my side of the shop. A chime rang out that was different from the door near where Brittany manned her own register. Seeing as she hadn't made an appearance yet, she was more than likely on break. Meaning she wouldn't be back in the front of the store unless told to by our manager, Natasha. And Nat was out on a supply run as our order had been short this morning on a few things, including the vacuum Brittany broke on Saturday.

Helmet turned opposite from where I had been attempting to buff a hole in the tabletop, I took the small advantage I was blessed with, darting for the counter. Clipping the counter with my hip, I sucked in my breath and the fuck that wanted to escape. Customer service smile on, hands ready to take his order, reminding myself to breathe, I stood poised to be as forgotten as his last left turn.

He may have been straight out of every dark romance book over on those shelves of glossy black that I had devoured as soon as they were placed for public viewing, but I wasn't the girl to get the guy. No matter what those authors wrote.

Too tall at five feet eight inches. The only curves I had were my hips, ass and thighs that I hid behind my baggy company issued black pants. And those had been commented on more than I liked since they were in disproportion to my C cup breasts. What worked for those girls songs like *I Like Big Butts* were sung about didn't fit with my plain brown hair that was pin straight and unmemorable plain blue eyes. Add in my lack of talent with makeup and large clear frame glasses, and I was just me.

Normally, I was okay with that. But not with Brittany the peppy, petite cheerleader with the T&A to match on the opposite register from me or mister sex wrapped in leather walking towards me. Hands with long fingers grabbed the helmet and pulled. Every scene from my latest read flashed in my head. Yeah, he was chapter three alright.

"Chapter three?"

Fuck, I'd said that out loud. Eyes, the shade of the beans I freshly roasted and ground this morning, were all I got to focus on and I was kind of shit at eye contact. He had yet to remove the full face covering some riders wore under their helmets.

"Yeah, sugar, you did."

And I'd said that out loud too. Face that had to be tomato red if the heat I was experiencing was any factor, I dropped my eyes to the marker in my fingers, ready to write his order on the side of his choice of cup. With a sigh, I attempted to fix my smile, "what can I get you today? We have just released our seasonal pumpkin spice back into the menu."

3

Gruff and grumpy, he looked over the menu behind me. "Sure, extra pump of caramel, french roast, vanilla milk, iced, whip, largest one you got."

This I could do. Snatching the corresponding cup, I ticked boxes, writing instructions for no one other than myself. Setting it down, I punched in his order to the register, "would you like any of our baked goods? I made the banana nut muffins fresh this morning and the rest yesterday."

With a shake of his head, he tapped his phone on the reader when it chirped at him. No tip. Before lifting those deep eyes back to me he looked around once more at the empty shop. Darting to the sink to avoid their depths, I washed my hands while humming twinkle twinkle twice. Snagging his cup, I began his order. I paused at frothing his milk of choice when he spoke behind me.

"Chapter three. Want to tell me the title that has you picturing me naked?"

Embarrassment filled my face with color again, stealing my voice so I couldn't answer if I wanted to.

"Kind of quiet here. I thought with all that stuff on social media about bookshops being the new bars, there would be...more."

Deep breath in, slow exhale, "this is the lull in the storm. It will pick back up. And it is midweek. Most serious readers don't pick up new material until at least Thursday, but mostly Friday. Can't be deep diving into whatever world they prefer with work looming the next day."

"I was in here last week. Met this little blonde thing who tried to help me find a book."

And that will be what I blamed on what I did next.

Grabbing the caramel and his cup, I pushed my back to the door to my left before darting inside. "I need a new bottle, be right back."

Pulling the necklace my Gram gave me from the neckline of the teal polo under my coffee brown apron, I looked at the little vial dangling from the end. At one time, I was sure it was for coke if the tiny spoon that popped out when you unscrewed the top was any indication. I kept something else in it.

My brain was screaming at me that this was wrong. My heart was yelling the word 'mine' in the voice of cartoon seagulls. Needless to say, my heart was steering this ship.

Dumping the powdered contents into the bowl on the counter, I squirted the caramel in and stirred until it was gone. Drizzling it into the cup, I stepped back out and finished assembling his drink. With a small smile, I handed it over to him. "Any of the books in the dark romance section about men who ride motorcycles like yours will more than likely catch your attention if you are looking for something like my latest read."

Fingers prepared to pull up his mask, he looked over at the stacks. "And which one are you reading?"

I couldn't read him. Was he being a jerk or honestly interested? Brittany may work that side but a reader she was not. She did read the blurbs so could steer a person in a general direction. But he didn't sound like he had bought anything. And then there was the comment about those videos. Was he looking for a hook up? "You can't miss it. It is on the end cap to the section. This month's featured read."

With a nod, he pulled his phone from a pocket on his leg as it vibrated hard enough to be heard. Turning his back to me he leaned on the counter in front of me, pushing the black fabric up on one side, thumb flying while he slurped his drink down to half in seconds.

Back in the room that was my haven from the bustle that work could be, I counted to twenty real slow. Popping my head out the swinging door, I called out to him. "Um, could you give me a hand. Please."

Phone shoved back in his pocket, setting his drink next to the tip jar, mask back in place due to the elasticity, he gave an eyeroll before rounding the corner of the counter. Just as he pushed the door in, he staggered, catching himself on the counter. Hand to his head, he closed and popped open his eyes in a way that told me he was trying to clear his vision. Taking his arm, I gave a tug, steering him to the cart I used to bring in loads of beans and supplies. "Are you okay?"

Deep brown eyes blinked up at me, each dip of his lashes slower before they closed. Guiding him down, I draped him on the bags of coffee I had yet to unload. Tucking him in so he didn't slide off as I pushed him to the lift we used to move things to and from the basement, I couldn't help the smile that graced my lips. "Yeah, just like chapter three."

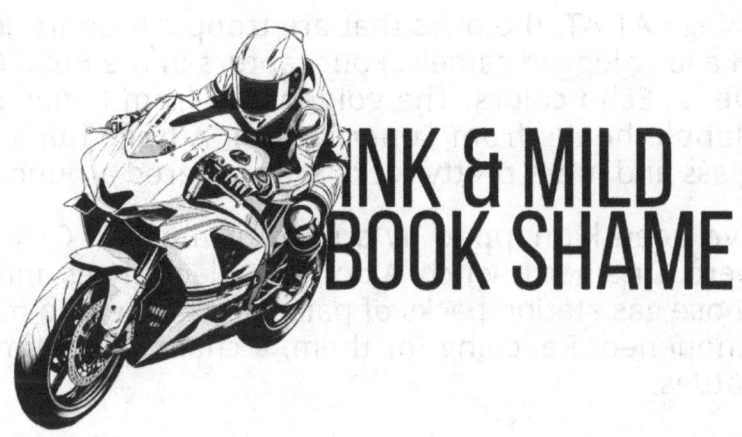

INK & MILD
BOOK SHAME

Tucker

"What in the ever loving fuck?" My face is smashed into plush carpeting in a deep shade of blue. Rolling my forehead into the weave of it, I pray that it will help the pounding of the drums that beat a bass line in my brain. Slowly opening my eyes, I wince at the same time I am thankful that the lighting is low. Lids closed, counting to ten, I pry them back open, turning my head to the right from where it is buried in the vanilla smelling rug.

Across from me is a bookshelf in progress with half the books in stacks on the floor in front of it. On the wall next to it, in front of a window covered in some kind of balloon looking see-through curtains, is a low backed couch in purple. Pillows and a throw give it an inviting feeling. Raising my head, I turn to the other wall. Facing me is a large hardwood desk with two monitors on it and a very comfortable looking chair behind it.

Pushing up on my arms, praying to anyone who will listen I don't vomit, I twist to look behind me. An electric fireplace is centered in another bookcase. This one is made of thick black pipe with the boards balanced on them from floor to ceiling. Books, books, and more books fill the room. Stationed among the collection are odd pieces of brik-a-brac. Dust collectors my grandma called them.

7

A lego AT-AT, the ones that are troop transport and look like long legged camels. Four raptors in the Beta, Charlie, Delta, Echo colors. The golden idol from Indiana Jones. Bobble heads from Supernatural. A huge hunk of lava glass and more pretty rocks are scattered around.

I've been kidnapped by a nerd or a witch. Or a witchy nerd. Or a nerdy witch. A bottle of electrolytes and one of those gas station packs of pain killers is next to me. Both unopened. Reaching for them, a chain around my wrist rattles.

My boots are gone, leaving me in my socks and riding suit. Pockets are empty. Helmet gone but my balaclava is in place. A little crooked from my rolling around into the carpet but I'm pretty much covered still from head to toe.

Examining the cuff on my arm, I pull at the material it is made out of. It reminds me of something but I can't place my finger on it. Soft material with a spongy feel but not enough to slip off. Wrapped around that to secure it closed is velcro. What keeps me shackled is the thick D ring pair. A lock connecting them to the chain next to me and unless I can find something to hack at it with.

Eyeing up the items left next to where my head was laying, I debate trusting them. I was drugged, obviously. But not dead. Tongue sticking to the roof of my mouth from whatever I was given, I decided the hell with it and reached for them.

Chugging the drink with the meds, I just listen. No air con kicks on to disturb the peace of the early fall evening if the fading light from the window is a measurement of time. In fact, I hear nothing from outside. No birds or traffic. I have to be above ground. A tree outside with more branches than trunk is visible through the window, blowing in the wind that was supposed to pick up this evening tells me so.

Overwhelming need to call out almost has a shout nearly tripping from me. But in doing so, I could alert whoever owns this house.

A sound muffled from the closed door has me freezing in my attempt to stand. Sitting back down, I close my eyes in an attempt to focus on what I heard. There. Pots clanging. Someone is cooking. Or at least I hope that is what that sound is. Sniffing, I try to block the scent of vanilla and spice the room holds. Someone is cooking. Smells like chicken. Fried. And fresh bread. Something sweet too, maybe for dessert.

I hope this isn't a basket and hole moment and those smells making my stomach growl will be shared. What can I say, I'm hungry. And since I'm still alive, and in a room that blood splatter would be hell to clean, I'm assuming I'm to be kept that way. Time ticks on with only the smell to tease me as the window darkens farther.

Before I can cast my thoughts into the ether that I'm not left here with only that delicious aroma to tease me, there is a muffled clinking of dishes. The deadbolt turning in the thick timber of the door isn't really comforting as the way to unlock it must be on the other side from me. Nothing to keep whoever took me out, but isn't that what kidnapping is about?

My brain supplies the only thing it seems it can at the moment, so again, what the ever loving fuck.

Desk blocking her from where I'm sitting all I can tell is she is tall for a woman when the world tells them they need to be petite, she comes in with a tray balanced in her hands. Steam comes from it as she sets it on the desk, turning to close the door. The sound of an automatic lock dashes any current plans to attempt escape even if my chain was long enough.

Without a word, she pads across the carpet in thick socks, setting the tray on the low table in front of the small couch. A flat square cushion is plunked down on the floor in front of it. I get a good look at her as she turns and sets on the end farthest from the food.

HOLY FUCKING SHIT!!

The girl from the bookstore!

"Hungry? It is close to seven, I'm sure you are. The last thing you had was that coffee before lunch. Eating will help the headache." A bottom heavy mouth gives a small smile, just a turn up of one side as she waits on some response from me.

I can feel the growls as my body screams for the food waiting for me. Like the drink and meds, I mentally toss my hands in the air. This could be my last meal for all I know. Scooching across to the cushion, I look down at the offering that has my stomach rumbling. A bowl of butter sits next to those little brown loaves of bread I love from that australian themed restaurant. A bowl of green beans with diced bacon on the other side of the tray. In the middle of them is a thick slice of chocolate cake. On a large plate in front of me is a mound of fluffy mashed potatoes dosed in a white gravy with flecks of pepper in it. Next to that is a thick slab of chicken. For it to be that thin, she had to have pounded it with a meat hammer before frying it up to a crispy golden battered perfection.

"I promise it isn't drugged or poisoned. I have my own plate waiting for me in the kitchen. I wanted to take this moment and give you the first rule. I don't want to see your face. Please use any method you like to keep it covered."

Cocking an eyebrow she can't see due to the fabric over my head, I can't help the little bit of snark that leaks out when I know I should play nice until I know what is what. "So rule one isn't no escaping but to keep my face hidden? Afraid I'll be ugly and not worth all your hard work?"

With a small smile, she stands and leaves. The door locks behind her.

I WRITE THE RULES

Ruby

I watch as he sniffs the food again. Cutting a piece of chicken, he actually licks it before shoving it into his mouth. He followed the face cover rule, pulling it up to only expose his mouth so he could eat. With a moan that has me pressing my thighs together, he dives in.

While I was dishing up our dinners, I watched him like I'm doing now on the television I have in the kitchen for the weather while I eat breakfast or late night baking. He took in the whole of the room around him, missing the cameras tucked into the corners and shelves that gave me plenty of angles.

He is perfect. I couldn't have written a better character. Chapter by chapter, he fits my plan. Rubbing my hands on my thighs now covered in suede soft leggings, I push the feel of him and his body from my memory so I can properly hold my fork and not wear my dinner. Just moving him, making sure he was restrained, it made me want things I will not ask of him.

I didn't do anything to him other than a pat down to find his phone and wallet. Those are now locked in a drawer in my desk. This is the part I hate. Seeing how long it will take him to leave. They all do. But I've learned a thing or two.

The chain will get him all around the room he is in and just into the adjoining bath. But only to the toilet, tub, and sink, not to the door leading to my room. His helmet is already in its spot on the shelves above his head where he hasn't noticed it. He is welcome to wear it. And if things progress, I might ask him to put it on.

Finishing my dinner, I move back down the short hall to the office door. Rapping my knuckles on the wood I call through, "please make sure your face is covered, I'm coming in to get the tray."

A slow count to five, I press the code into the pad and the deadbolt thunks open.

He is sitting on the floor still. The tray is empty except for the dishes, all items accounted for. I left him without any more to drink to encourage him to find the bathroom. He doesn't say anything as I take my seat back on the sofa. "Ready for the rest of the rules?"

Damn if he doesn't actually growl at me and I can't help the giggle that slips out.

"One, keep your face covered at all times. The only times you can remove it is for a shower or in complete darkness."

Another growl has me clenching my thighs again. "Why?"

He had asked the first time why and I hadn't answered. I couldn't keep avoiding it, even if the thought of him leaving already twisted my guts in knots. "Because when you leave, and we run into each other around town, you don't have to acknowledge me and I won't know who you are. Less awkward for you, you know?"

I take the silence as he digests my round about reason for the mask to continue.

"Two, freedom is earned."

Eyes can be so expressive if that is all you have to read on a person's face and his are saying he is curious what he has to do to earn that freedom.

He doesn't take the opportunity to ask so I go on. "Three, no yelling. Won't do you any good. The walls are thick due to the age of my house and I've had it upgraded. It isn't soundproof but unless someone is standing right outside it, they won't hear anything. And no one has reason to or lives close enough to do that."

Silence as he waits for me to go on. But three is all he gets. Keep it simple so there is no need for forgetfulness. With a huff, he looks around the room again before those deep brown eyes meet mine. "Where's my bike?"

With a tick of my head in the direction it is, I answer him, "in the garage."

He scratches his neck, pushing the cloth out of the way, as he gives the room another quick look. He will go over every inch as soon as I leave him for the night as I know. It is common sense to look for a weapon or way to break out. And since I don't want to be brained with a book or anything else, I'll check the cameras before entering each time.

Finally, he asks about rule two. "How? How do I earn my freedom?"

Standing, I look over the tray. The fork has a bent tine. I look at him with an arched brow, earning me a shrugged shoulder. "Follow the rules."

Balancing the tray on my arm, I press my thumb to the sensor on this side of the door.

"For how long?"

Looking back over my shoulder, I return his shrug before leaving him for the night.

I watch as I wash the dishes as he moves around the room, chain dragging. Hefting heavy items to test their viability as a weapon. Anything that can be used as a key or pick is tested on the lock. The desk is picked over and when none of the drawers open, abandoned. He is spinning back and forth in the chair when he gets up to move to the second door in the room.

When he sees the bathroom, he returns for the drink bottle. The cameras follow his movements from one room to the other. He fills the bottle with water, drinks it down, refills it again before looking around this room too.

Nothing but bathroom necessities greets him as he looks in the cabinet next to the shower. Towels, extra bottles of soap and shampoo. A new toothbrush is on the counter, still in the packaging. Toilet paper, pads, and tampons greet him under the sink.

He won't find even a stray bobbie pin. All that is kept in my other bathroom. Lesson learned on that one. Fingers stretching, he fumbles the other door that is just in his reach in the room before getting it open.

Hmmm, he has a longer wingspan than I thought. Should have shortened up his tether with a factor to those long limbs and lean muscles.

Bed, neatly made in the new terracotta comforter I got last week. The white frame pops against the earthen orange and deep grey. If he could see more he would find a long dresser to the left of the door. End tables on each side of the bed. My closet full of comfortable clothes and work uniforms. Another bookshelf like he is tied to. Nothing personal like pictures. Nothing to tell him who I am but a nerd who likes to read. A lot.

He moves back to the office. Growling, he stands in the middle, arms crossed over his chest as he looks around. Pushed in the corner next to the couch is a small trunk.

Guess he was expecting it to be locked as the lid smacks the wall when he lifts the leather handle, having him looking around to see if that counted as breaking rule three.

That is when he notices a camera. Quickly followed by the others. Not that I hid them, they just don't have blinking red lights that scream 'here we are'.

Shaking his head, he looks down to see if he found anything good.

Depends on who you are asking. A mat like those used by campers that gives some protection from the floor. A couple blankets and pillows. Each in different weight. Sleep pants and a tee. He flips me off as he goes into the bathroom. I turn from the camera to give him the privacy he doesn't know he is getting, listening to the sounds to know he is changing clothes.

The crinkle of the plastic covering the toothbrush, lets me know he has changed. His suit is tossed over the top of the shower door, leaving him in his tank and the thin sleep pants. Where the sleeves were tied around his waist from before he entered the coffee shop made that part easy on me. It would have been like wrestling an octopus to get him out of it if I had had to do it on my own.

I can't help the smile at him standing barefoot in my home, brushing his teeth.

HELP ME BRUH

Ruby

Earlier That Day

Sweat runs down my back and soaks my underwear as I shut the back door to the shop. Chuckling at my own inner thoughts of hauling my prize back to my lair, I take a moment to lean back against the door, panting. Even with the cart, his weight was barely manageable.

What few know is that our little sleepy town used to be a stop on the railroad. Prohibition saw those tunnels being put to use again. My house was a distillery and warehouse, connecting to the older part of town. The basement here was a speakeasy. Most think the tunnels are sealed. Some are. But this one isn't. Cleverly hidden behind a faux wall in case either end was raided in time when alcohol was illegal. Now I use them. My home is set at the end of a block with a little more land than the others to have some privacy to it. My only complaint, it is uphill. I need to install a winch or some kind of pulley system. The overstock of books I keep aren't doing my muscles any favors if I am left like this each time.

And then moving his bike from out front to the shelter around the dumpster until I can get it home on top of it, whew. I didn't think it would be that heavy and I hate to admit I almost dropped it twice. If I laid it over on its side,

17

there would be no way to get it back up, thank whichever god or goddess was listening earlier that they granted me the strength to move that blacked out beast.

"Ruby?!"

Head back against the door, I heave a sigh. Of course Brittany would need me before I can catch my breath. Stepping to the small sink for handwashing, I push a few escaped strands of hair back behind my ears. The pink cheeks I can't do anything about. Snatching paper towels like I would love to do to the perfect blonde beach curls of the person now shoving open the swinging door, I dry my hands.

"Didn't you hear me?" Okay, she doesn't look pissed, more...giddy. "You're needed. You know I can't work all those machines."

No, she doesn't want to. Part of her training was learning to run the café side of the business in the case the person on that side needed help. All I heard the whole time I attempted to teach her even a basic drink was that the steam frizzed her hair, she was chipping her manicure, the smell of coffee made her stink, the heat made her makeup run. I could write a novel with the complaints she lobbed my way. And it wasn't just this side she complained about. Unboxing books was a whine fest too.

Stepping around her, I pulled up short at the crowd waiting for me. Were they Mogwai? Did I splash water on the one I just ferried out of here? No less than seven more leather clad riders were in front of the counter, looking over the menu or leaving fingerprints on the glass of my display case.

"See, I told you all I'd find her for you. Now when you get your drinks and snacks, come see me." Wiggling her fingers, Brittany retreated to lean on her counter, not bothering to hide the fact she was ogling the men in front of me. Not even the promise of all this walking eye candy would keep her here for fear I would put her to work.

Clearing my throat, I drew every set of eyes my way. Not the way that Brittany did as she walked away, but in a no-nonsense way that I was no more important than the equipment behind me. "What can I get you?" I gave the same spiel I gave the man tied in my office. "We just brought back our pumpkin spice if any of you are interested."

Helmets were scattered on the biggest table, necks covered in the face protection they wore under them as it was warm in here. Shooting Brittany a look around them, I figured she hiked up the thermostat to get them to take something off.

Kitted out in a red, black, and white ensemble, the one closest to me stepped up to order. One after the other placed iced drink orders, most with pumpkin spice. Cookies, muffins, brownies, cupcakes. All in jumbo sizes since I felt if you were going to order drinks that would ruin any diet with all the sugar in them, why not finish it off with a snack to soak up all that caffeine, flew out of the case.

Dining in meant that they got actual mugs and dishes. Pulling a tray from under the counter, I wiped it off since I knew they weren't used that often, I filled it with their order. They took up the side that was one long vinyl booth seat with tables and chairs in front of it. As I handed out their orders, I listened to what they were talking about. They had to be with my unwilling guest, if not this was the worst case of coincidence ever.

"Still no answer. He said this one, right?" The one talking twirled his finger at the room around them.

Nodding with a whip topping mustache, the guy across and two seats down answered, "yup. He confirmed it this morning when he reminded us all about meeting up here."

Cheeks bulged out like a chipmunk with the huge bite of brownie he just shoved in, another one mumbled out, "I got shit to do and this looks like a bust."

"We've been here five minutes and it is a Wednesday." Thumbs flying over his phone, one dressed in more lime green than even Shego wears, paused long enough to look up at me when I set his latte down. "Wait, you work here?"

Laughter filled the space at his rhetorical question. Looking down at my rumpled uniform and back at Mister Shego, I shrugged as I tucked the tray under my arm. "Not really. I just do this as a sociological experiment."

Coughing and thumping follows my answer as another one chokes on his food. Once he can breathe, he points his finger at me, "*Me, Myself, and Irene* reference! She's fucking awesome."

"I was going to ask her advice until you dicks turned it into a laugh fest," Mister Shego leans back in the booth seat with a pout on his face.

Plastering on my best customer service face, I give him my full attention. "What can I help you with, sir?"

Snorts from those around us at the title have him flipping his companions off. "You know how social media says that book girls are hidden freaks and the best place to get them are libraries and book stores?"

I nod with a sigh, waving my hand for him to go on. That confirmed it, since he mentioned the same social media trends, my guest was with them.

"Well, we were trying to see if it was true. We were supposed to meet a friend here and he is a no show, unless you saw a tall thin dude in all black with a bike to match?"

Oh, I saw him. But I have the *best* poker face. "Thin dude?" Tall? Yes. Thin? No. He is solid if the weight of him and pushing that cart was any indication. I couldn't lift him or even pull him without wheels assisting. I had to roll him to unload him in my own basement and was glad for the helmet

20

when it bounced off the floor when gravity and momentum took over. And let's not talk about me squishing him into the dumbwaiter and dragging him from it to his room. "No. But you said it yourself. You need to time your visit."

I got all eyes on me, hanging on my every word like I'm parting some great knowledge. Since they seem pretty chill, I play on it, letting my actual self out. Looking around like someone might be spying on us, I motion them all closer. "So, I'm not supposed to be telling you this, reader code, girl code, and all that, but it's all true. But there are a few things you need to know first."

Mister Shego looks like he is about to bust out and take notes.

Another shifty eyeball of the shop and I lay it on thick, lowering my voice so they have to really lean in. I can see Brittany out of the corner of my eye, trying to listen in to what I'm saying but her area is too far from this one. "Ok, so we all want to act out those scenes but consent. Always get permission before you chase someone through the woods."

The looks on their faces almost have me laughing out loud. Head nods and shared looks clearly say I'm speaking some kind of higher truth.

"Two, read the books. The whole thing. Not just the spicy scenes. They are going to want to talk about *everything* about the story."

This is met with groans and cursing. They thought this was going to be easy.

"Sorry, got to read the books. Or you can do audio. There is more to them than smut. Well, some of them are more spice than plot."

This turns their frowns upside down.

"Number three might be a little controversial but, try books other than those that are mainstream. Pick up something other than what everyone is talking about. You can read those too, but be diverse. Readers do it and so should you."

More nods of agreement.

I look around, see Brittany pretending to dust to see what is going on and jerk my head in her direction. They all scoot closer together and to me. "Timing. You can't catch what isn't there. Most readers pick up a new book on Friday. That way they can read without worrying about work. You need to check launch dates and times. Signings. New books are the draw for readers. We do ours on the second Thursday at seven for a launch and the fourth Saturday for signings. They get a discount in the café when they buy one of the new books. We will get them in the door, you just got to show up."

They all lean back. Talking among themselves. Either I just got some new customers or unleashed some creepy dudes on my customers. Hmm, better warn them about that.

"Let me give you one last piece of advice. You're going to be stared at. Objectified. But most will find you creepy, especially if you keep the helmet on for too long. So if who you are chatting up ignores you. Move on. If they stare but don't speak. Move on. If they respond, give them your number. But move on. And do all this politely. No rude comments or you might end up on the wrong end of a booktoker. And if they can't think it up, most read things to draw inspiration from."

Uneasy laughter followed me back to the counter where I cleaned up the mess made while getting their orders. My counters were spotless when the tray I had set down on a table and forgotten reappeared next to the register with their cups and plates stacked neatly. Hefting it, I backed into the swinging door, I nodded to their waves, "thank you Mister Shego for bringing the tray back."

More laughter and back slapping as he joined his crew followed by the revving of engines.

I needed to get that bike to the house tonight. Since Brittany never did the trash haul, I was safe until I could get it moved.

Tucker

I'm coming out of the bathroom as another tray is set on the coffee table. The smell of bacon fills the room. Fluffy scrambled eggs, biscuits, and hash browns fill this plate. A glass of orange juice and a mug of coffee waits for me.

Seated across from me is my kidnapper on another one of those square cushions. Her own plate and orange juice in front of her, hair in one of those fluffy balls on top of her head. A tank covered in a sweater I think they call a cardigan, pajama shorts in a flannel looking material that looks soft and well worn. Thick socks hide her feet. "Morning?"

From the tone, I know she is fishing for my name. I know hers thanks to the nametag yesterday. No reason not to give it to her. She could know it already if she had looked in my wallet but I got this strange feeling she didn't. The need to keep my face covered tells me she is respecting my identity. Strange, but okay. I could give her a fake name but my own rolls off my tongue. "Tucker. Morning."

I've had many meals with the opposite sex but this one takes the cake. Breakfast with my kidnapper. As she eats her bacon, she hums happily, giving a little dance on her pillow. The sun is filtering in those gauzy curtains, haloing her in golden light. Face free of make up, I can see everything that makes her who she is on the outside.

Hair the color of the perfect coffee and milk combo. Eyes a darker shade of blue than the sky outside. Light dusting of freckles on her nose and cheeks. Braless breasts that would make the perfect handful. And that ass. Makes me want to bite it and then wrap those thick thighs around my hips as I pound into her. A trickle of butter from her biscuit drips down her hand, which she follows with her tongue. My dick kicks in my pants.

Well, that was interesting. Pausing with my coffee at my lips. I gave her another look over. A small tattoo trails from behind her left ear down under the shoulder of her sweater. It looks like birds but not quite. A chain around her neck holds a pendant of tiger's eye. I know that one as I was given a worry stone once made of it. Her tits are wrapped in a tank of orange with black kittens tumbling all over it. Her nipples are hard.

Down boy. I need to have a talk with my cock. He does not need to be interested in the woman who obviously drugged me and chained me up in her library. Change of subject. "Did you ride my bike?"

She is tall enough to have handled it but I still worry what I will find when I get out of here, if I get out of here. Shaking her head, she takes a quick sip of juice before answering me. "Pushed it. It was a lot heavier than I thought it would be. Don't worry. I didn't hurt it."

Trying to figure out where I am, I ask, "how far did you have to move it?"

"Hmm? Oh, a couple blocks." She was busy making a bacon and egg skewer out of her fork to pay attention to what she said. Not that it was helpful.

Having lived here my whole life, there are places that I just don't come to. So I prod a little more. "Not uphill the whole way I hope?"

Her answer to that will tell me at least in what direction I am. One side of town has a slope to it, nearly all residential but it does that behind the bookstore and the block it sits on. She nods. "The whole way, took me a bit. Made me wish I knew how to ride but I got it here."

Okay. Big house, older. Secluded. Uphill from town itself. Not an exact pin in the map but a narrowed search area. Her breakfast is gone and with nothing to distract her, I look around for something else to keep her talking.

When I had woke up this morning, I noticed on the shelf above me, a set of helmets. Men's from the sizing. Mine sat next to them. Buffed from finger prints. The matte black of it in contrast to the glossy red of one and the scuffed surface of the white and blue. Turning, I nodded to them when I felt her eyes on me. "What about those?"

The sharp click of stacked plates followed by the clink of glassware, told me she was cleaning up the dishes before I turned back to her. The look on her face didn't match the smile. I could tell it was forced. Her eyes were sad, rimmed in tears. At the door, she stopped to look at the shelf. "They didn't stay."

ANNOTATIONS ON A READER'S HEART

Tucker

Placing another book back on the shelf. I shake my head at the conclusion I have come to. Sex. That is why I'm here. The theme in the books is normally the man is the aggressor. Taking the poor helpless heroine for the purpose of some form of sexual need. As she has not said anything about a ransom. Her rules. The other helmets. She has flipped the script, become the kidnapper, and now wants...

Sex.

It has to be. But how does she plan to do it?

Drugging me again?

Coercing me in some manner?

That one makes sense. In exchange for letting me go.

I haven't seen her all day except once. She must have the day off as she appeared in a pair of work coveralls tied around her waist and a stained tee, smelling of saw dust with a sandwich and chips for lunch. No words spoken, just laid them on the corner of the desk and left.

Deadbolt clicking, I watch as the panel opens and a sight that stops me in my tracks fills the door. Holy fuck but a woman in a tool belt equals instant boner. I watch as she measures the empty space on the opposite wall where I'm chained. It is when she starts taking more books down, stacking them next to the couch, that I'm prompted into movement. Spontaneous aide. A new symptom of Stockholm?

Soon the area is clear and that is when the power tool comes out. As she is taking a board down that is slightly above her head, I have to dive to catch it from smacking her in the face. Pressed to her back, I can feel the sweat of her work through the tee she is wearing. Looking down from where I'm holding the wood, I realize my own is nestled right in her ass.

Head turning, eyes the color of my favorite denim jacket meet mine. All those shades of blue a well loved and worn piece of Levi's stare at me. It is the flick of that pink tongue on her lips that snaps my control. Shoving the bottom of my head cover up like I do when I eat, I pounce.

Thoughts of being used for exactly this flee. She did nothing to seduce me other than be able to handle power tools and work up a sweat.

Ruby

Tucker's lips crash onto mine, taking my breath. From zero to a hundred. I drop my drill as I turn in his arms, threading my own around his neck. The board crashes behind me when he lets go to grab my ass and lift me so my legs wrap around his waist.

He didn't bother putting his one piece riding suit back on so the pajamas I left him are a thin barrier to his dick as he grinds it into my pussy. Steps backwards bringing us to the couch in front of the window and we are falling as he sets down.

Hands move, stripping shirts over heads. My bra is dropped on the cushion next to us. Calluses rasp over my flesh as he slides his palms up my sides to cup under my tits, lifting them to feast on.

Hot tongue swirling around my nipples, teeth on the tightly puckered tips. Then suction. Damn, I can feel that between my legs. Each pull a pulse. Leaning back, I plant my hands on his knees, offering myself as a bounty to feast on. I can't help the grind of my hips on Tucker's lap.

Cursing the thick coveralls that keep me from feeling him the way I need, I sit back up. I can't get to his hair to steer him where I want due to the face covering he promised to not take off, I wrap my hand around his neck and use the space between my thumb and first finger to tilt his head back. Smashing my lips to his, tongues dueling, I stand and untie the sleeves holding the bottom half to my waist.

Large hands join mine, pushing the fabric down my thighs. Toeing off my boots, he plants a foot in the middle of the pile around my ankles to help me step out. Fingers grab my underwear on my hips, pulling them just as quickly down and off.

Back in his lap, I look into the only part of his face I can see. Those deep eyes. "I'm on the shot. I'm clean. I can get a condom."

Those calluses rough against my cheek, Tucker cups my jaw, his thumb rubbing my cheek. "We will do whatever you want. I'm clean. Got tested last month after a break up.'

Raising up on the knees planted on either side of his hips, I drop my mouth back down on his. Hands fumbling, we both work at pushing his pants down.

The cock that appears at being given its freedom has my mouth watering. I'm not a size queen but a girl that does like a little more. Flushed a blushed peach color, head a darker shade. Trimmed hair, balls drawn up already.

Sliding off the couch. I kneel between his legs, wrapping a hand around his base, I aim the tip at my lips. Licking the drop that seeps from the slit, I hum my approval, shimmying my hips at the way it makes me happy to see him throw back his head, hissing a breath as I suck him down. Hands settle on either side of my head, not making me take more, just holding on as I bob up and down his length. With a slurp, I pull off, using my spit to make the pump of my fist glide smoother. He gives another grunt as I tighten my fingers around the length growing darker, thicker.

I'm scooped under my arms and deposited back on his lap. His cock gives a twitch at not having attention before he fist is circling the base to hold it steady as he pulls on my hip to get me to rise. Tucker rubs the head between the lips of my pussy, coating him in the wet that seeps from me.

Notching at my opening, he wraps those long fingers over my hips, thumbs pressing into my hip bones, skin dimpling in a way that says later I'll have bruises, he pulls me down. Gasps leave us both as he slides in.

Eyes so dark they look black stare at me while I settle on his lap. Leaning back again, hands on his knees, I roll my hips. The drag and fill has me dropping my head back. Fingers digging in, a growl rumbles from his throat as he pulls me down faster, harder.

I'm reaching for my own clit, balance precarious, when Tucker beats me there. Thumb pressing, rubbing. I cry out as the world goes fuzzy at the edges.

The word fuck is growled out as he holds me to him, pulsing inside me shortly after my walls grab onto the length moving inside me. Panting, I drape myself over his chest, damp breath on my ear matches mine feathering across his neck.

EVEN VAMPIRES NEED YARD TIME

Tucker

Laying on the floor, I stare up at a chandelier, gold and crystals reflect the light onto every surface, rainbows twinkling over the spines of her books. It fits her. Well, what little I know about her.

I woke this morning to the cuff open next to me. It took my brain longer than I would have liked to realize that I was free. Partially. After it clicked I wasn't going to be dragging a chain around like a specter in a remake of a Dickens' tale as Marley's ghost, I examined every knob I had access to. Locked up tighter than Fort Knox.

Wait...

The window doesn't open. The bathroom door is closed. There isn't a fan or anything like that on. And the heat hasn't kicked on for a while. Glad for that last one as it is stuffy in here with an unusually sunny day. Regretting the fact I dressed back into my one piece after my mad dash for attempted escape. I'm sweating my balls off. But this new focus puts my dripping nuts from my mind.

Studying the swaying glass, I follow what should be the direction the air is coming from. Head cocked like a patient hound, I move to the corner to the left of the bare shelves we emptied. These are original, framing the window. Thick in a way that says the walls in places might not be what they seem.

Hand out like I'm trying to Vader someone into compliance, I concentrate on what I feel or don't.

There!

A very small breath of air from a seam in the shelves where the corner meets. Stepping back, I examine all in the vicinity of that scent of freedom. Tapping books, lifting bric-a-brac, I nearly shout out loud when I try to pick up a little brass frog and it is attached. Looking around, I know she can see me but I haven't seen her since breakfast and she left lunch in an insulated cooler bag. It is now or never. I don't know how fast she can get here but if I can get out, I assume the game is over.

Pushing the frog and lifting it didn't do anything. I pinch its head and go to wiggle it when it rocks back on its back legs. Such a clever design, I can't help to take a moment to look over the seamless way he blends right in.

With a smile and wave at the camera, I step into the dark opening. Motion activated lights around knee level glow as I check out where I am. A passage between the inner and outer walls. I could tell the house was old but this is awesome.

At a T juncture, I pause to try to think about where I am and what I could see out the windows.

"Left."

I nearly piss myself when her voice comes from around me. How close is this house to town? She said it was private so there is no way she could have got here that fast. I set off to the right, common sense says to go the opposite.

"Tsk, tsk, tsk. This is why one of the rules isn't to escape. Basic human drive is to do just that. Remove a freedom and we will do whatever we can to get it back."

I can tell from the puff in her breathing she is moving while she talks to me. I have maybe a few minutes to make it outside. Something in me says that to touch grass is the ultimate base in this cat and mouse game. Stairs at the next intersection go up or I can turn left. Up isn't where I need to be, I'm on the second floor now and need to go down.

Her laugh follows me past the narrow steps, "how predictable. You need to think outside the box."

Pausing, I look back at those narrow treads that go up to who knows where. I take them two at a time, coming out in an attic room. Maybe a servant's sleep area back when the previous owners were very well off and not a single woman working as a barista? Cold iron fills my hand, popping open but only a crack. I can see a hasp and padlock when I squint through. Fuck.

"If I find you, what do I win?"

Not bothering to examine where the voice is coming from, I keep moving as I answer her. "I'll go back to the library. But if I make it out of the house..."

A sigh comes at me in stereo. "If you make it out of the house, you are free to go. I'll give you your keys and wave to you as you ride off."

Pausing, I look around. The sadness in her voice almost has me retracing my steps back to my prison. Shaking my head, I look right at the camera pointing at me I missed when I came out of the wall, they must be all over, including in the wall passages. "Using the cameras isn't playing fair."

"You're right. Rules are for the fair play of games. I'm laying my phone here in the kitchen and then I'm coming for you." I could hear the smile as the sound of her breathing silenced in the feed.

Moving quickly, I focus on the end result. The wind as it tries to rip me from the back of my bike. Adrenaline as I take turns too fast. Speed pushing everything from my head. No noise. No hustle. No chains.

Down the set of stairs as I'm sure she went up since that was the last place she saw me, pausing at the bottom, I pick a direction at random. Light more pure than what is filling the space around me draws me to a small gap. Stopping, I dance my fingers in the soft beams coming from a crack near a small latch.

I swear I can smell the leaves that were falling from trees as fall settled in when I was taken. Moist ground preparing to go into the slumber of winter. Smoke from chimneys as fires are lit to ward the chill of autumn.

Pushing open the door, my shoulders slump, smile fading.

The office.

My jail cell.

And sitting behind her desk is my kidnapper.

"I think I'll let you shower. With all that dust on your skin, you look like a vampire in need of a good feed. The cobwebs say you just woke up from a long sleep." Corners of her mouth turning up in a smile, I don't answer, just go to the bathroom, stripping off my suit.

I feel her eyes on me as I reach in to adjust the water. "Left?"

I can see her shaking her head in the mirror, leaning on the door frame with her arms crossed over her stomach. More holding herself than in anger. Did my attempt upset her? She has to know I would attempt it. I step into the shower, pulling my mask off when my back is to her. "Would have taken you to the kitchen and the back door which lets out next to the garage and your bike."

PAGE TEN

Ruby

Am I upset?

Sure.

Who wouldn't be? The best fuck I've had that wasn't battery powered just tried to walk away. I knew he would try to escape. They all do. I got the alert on the door while in the middle of making a harried mom a giant iced latte. By the time I was able to duck out, he had come to the first intersection.

Why had I told him the way out?

I can't answer that. To myself or now that he asked. I just don't know. I normally would have taunted him into doing as he had done on his own. Picking up a new set of lounge pants and tee, I add some thick socks to the fabric gripped in my hands.

Setting it on the counter, I take a moment to look over the muscles as they move with his hands on his head, pushing the water from his hair. His mask is hanging with the towel I put over the top of the door.

Moving to the door opposite, I look over the room. He had been laying on the floor, staring up. Something caught his attention. The slight turn of one of the crystals hanging from the lighting fixture I had restored has me cocking my head. Soaking and scraping years of filth and paint, I had had little faith I could save it. I'd had to source missing pieces offline, hoping that I was getting something that matched each time I placed an order.

Following his steps, I stand in front of the shelf with the hidden door. I can feel the air that was just strong enough to make the teardrop on the end of the cascade dance. That would need to be plugged. Some rubber weather stripping would do the job.

The slap of water on the tile has me returning to the door. Keeping my eyes down so as not to see his face, I wait for the water to shut off so I can reattach the cuff. His voice has me jumping.

"What is your name?"

Like I gave him rules, I have some of my own. One is not to give my name unless asked. Sure, this house would be easy to find and he knows where I work and when he gets free. But names have power. I don't ask theirs and don't volunteer mine. But he *did* ask. "Ruby."

"Tucker."

Not knowing what else to say as the normal niceties of greeting sure don't apply here. Drugging. Kidnapping. Sex. Kind of past the 'nice to meet yous'.

"Come here Ruby."

I almost look up at the command. First, command. Hell no. I run this show. Second, command. Fuck yes. Deep voice pulling me in.

He must think my hesitation is due to the face covering rule, "close your eyes and join me. Please."

36

I couldn't resist if I tried. Eyes down, I pulled off my clothes. The door opened, steam filling the room. A large hand wrapped around my wrist, tugging me in.

"Are they closed?"

Nodding my head as lashes fanned down and my view of our feet disappeared. Cold had me arching as my back was pressed into the tile. Long fingers traced my jaw before cupping my face, tilting it for the lips that pressed to mine.

Kisses, nips, sucks trailed down my neck. Collar bones were traced with Tucker's tongue. The weight of my breasts was measured, hefted. Nipples pinched between the sides of his thumb and forefinger. Thunking my head back on the wall, I focused on the pain and the kiss of apology he placed on them when he released the pressure.

Down my stomach, that wicked tongue dipping into my belly button. Shoulders shoving at my thighs had me attempting to widen them as Tucker hit his knees for me. He was too tall even for my frame. Which found my leg tossed over his shoulder and hands cupping my ass, thumbs cradling my thigh creases to help me find my balance.

Mouth buried in my pussy. Clit being sucked so hard I saw stars I came, hard and fast. One of those hands slid forward, two fingers filling me to the beat of my orgasm and the sucks on my clit.

Threading my fingers into his hair, I pulled. "Please, just a second. Too sensitive."

Tucker let me have my break. Kisses pressed to my thigh over his shoulder. "Keep those eyes closed."

I almost looked as the shock of being empty when he slid his fingers free pulled me from the trance he had put me under. Feeling him as he stood, I gasped as I was spun around, hands slapping the wall to catch myself.

"Good girl." Growl rumbling in my ear, I couldn't help the shiver that raced down my spine. "On your toes, arch for me."

Hmm, I did as he said. It was my rule and game after all.

The heat coming off his cock felt searing where it rested against my ass. "Spread them."

His foot tapping my ankles, moving them out, was followed by his own palm planting next to mine on the wall. Nose trailing from my shoulder to my ear where he nipped the lobe. The push of that glorious cock into my waiting flesh had my forehead meeting the wall as I moaned into the steam surrounding us.

Pumping hips. Tucker worked in until he was as deep as he could get. With another growl, he sunk his teeth into that muscle that connects shoulder and neck. Holding position on my toes, legs spread to give him room, I panted into the wall. "Fuck, Tucker, move!"

A snorted laugh was my answer and he did as he was told. Hips plowed me to oblivion. The drag of his cock as he pulled, the pressure of the push. Huffs of deep breaths feathered over the side of my face. I wanted to see. See that pleasure as we got each other off. Fighting the urge to make eye contact, I arched my back, ass out to take as much of the cock plowing me as I could.

"Tucker, please." I was asking for more. More of him. More of right now. And he answered. Fingers moved around my hip and between my legs, finding my swollen clit. Rolling, pressing.

Those teeth returned to my skin. Dark spots danced as I screamed into the water that was fast fading from hot to cold as we ran the tank I was meaning to replace out. But it was worth it.

Tucker sat glaring at the cuff that was now around his ankle instead of his wrist. It would make doing daily things easier if he had both hands free. He didn't see it that way. All he saw was that he was tied again. Even if it was his fault. "This is bullshit. I'm sure you are going to secure that door and I can't get out of this room, the bathroom, or even into your bedroom."

The clicking of my keys is his only answer.

"Ruby, come on." Flicking my eyes from the screen I'm working on to those deep chocolate ones that attempt to snare me from my work, to find him looking at his foot propped on the corner of the coffee table and the padded cuff secured with a padlock and chain to the same pole that is the main support of the bookcase surrounding my electric fireplace.

I get ten minutes of peace before Tucker stands and walks over to look over my shoulder. I don't worry about what he may see or him getting access to the internet. I got it locked down and what I'm working on really isn't a secret.

"You're writing about us? This?" I don't bother looking up as I finish and save. I will illustrate it later from my tablet. Drawing on that is easier with my stylus.

"Patreon can be profitable. Graphic novels are growing in popularity." Clicks of my mouse have the screens going dark. The only way to wake them up now is the fingerprint scanner setting just under my monitor.

Looking up at Tucker, I take in his crossed arms and arched brow. Even with the mask on, I can tell he has that brat tamer brow. "Do I get a say in this?"

Nodding I reach for the top left drawer and pull out a piece of paper.

HARDCORE LORE

Ruby

Tucker braces his hands on my desk, arms locked. All that muscle and those juicy veins on display. I want to snatch up my markers and color in his tattoos. Koi fish, water splashes, and lotus flowers spiral up one. Dragons tangled together on the other.

The paper is simple. A non-disclosure with permission for me to use our experience in my art, with the players remaining anonymous. He signs, I sign. Scan to my lawyer and done.

Tapping the pen that I pulled out of the skinny drawer across my lap, I wait for him to digest what he is reading. And wait. And wait some more.

"What is this?" If I lean up a little, our lips would meet.

Clearing my throat and thoughts, I point with the pen to the top paragraph. "You cannot speak to anyone, except police or a therapist, about what happens here." Next paragraph, "I have permission to use anything that happens here, in any format, as long as your identity and mine remain obscured. Monetary compensation remains mine as the sole owner of any art created from our time together. Compensation cannot be sought for any profits made." Pen tapping the final paragraph with that part, I look up at him. Head covering back on, all I can see is his eyes. And they look a little confused.

"I can go to the cops. I can put you in jail."

If anything, his eyes look scared now. But of what? Me?

"Yes?"

"You didn't protect anything but what you plan to write? Why didn't you protect yourself?"

"It wouldn't matter. Any judge would throw that out."

Shaking his head, Tucker snatches the pen from my hand and signs and dates his lines. "So beside what I saw you working on, you got what? OnlyFans? PornHub? Some kind of kink website you load it up to? I'm sure there are people out there who get off on all this."

The wave of his hand as it encompasses the room as a whole almost has me messing up my own signature. Pulling out the large drawer on my left, I lift out the scanner. Powering it on, I wait for the chime from my room that says it is connected to my phone. I'll send the document through before I go to bed. I see the moment Tucker notices his phone in the drawer that is still open.

He walks around to lean on that side of the desk as we watch the paper feed from the other side of the slim machine. "Nope. Just the novels. I don't want to watch my ass jiggle anymore than the next person. I'll send this to my lawyer and we are done."

Squatting down, he looks me in the eyes when he delivers a statement that rings in truth even if I know it was a move to get his device. "I'd watch you anytime, all the time."

Flicking the paper back into the drawer it came from, I watched him palm his phone from the corner of my eye. Pretending to place the scanner by feel back into the drawer and shut it, I break eye contact. Once the drawers were all shut, I shoved the top middle all the way closed, activating the locking mechanism.

Part of this game was to see what he did in his attempts to seek freedom. Standing, I stretched, watching his eyes dance down over the cropped cami as it rode up even more. "I need to go grocery shopping. You got any requests?"

Eyes snap up from my tits I am sure were ready to pop out the bottom of my shirt. It takes a moment for his brain to catch up to his ears it seemed. "Um, I eat healthy or at least try to. Your food is good, great, but I'm used to..."

A smile curls the corner of my mouth as I wait for him to finish. With a wave of his hand and then a shrug, he moves to sit on the couch, using the adjustment of the throw pillow to hide him dropping his phone behind it. Subtle. "Got it. It's not like you can go to the gym or whatever you do. Just don't jump rope with the chain. I don't want you to break yourself or anything in here."

Tucker eyes the chain coiled on the floor. "Think I will stick with the floor program I've been doing."

With a wave over my shoulder, I turn to head to my own room. Laying in bed, I turn my television on to hide the glow of my phone as I watch him make his bed. Not once does he reach for the phone behind the pillow. Just goes about his routine of bed, lights, getting comfortable.

I'm nearly asleep when he sits up to adjust his pillow. As he reaches for the top of the pillow to change the angle, he quickly snags the phone. His hand under the pillow tells me he is powering it on even if I can't see the glow of it.

He must have it already set to a low light setting since I nearly miss the move as he pulls it from under the pillow to under the blanket. One arm is under the pillow like he normally sleeps, the other under the blanket where he must be typing out an SOS.

Tucker

I can't call for help. Something in me won't let me call the cops. Maybe it is that she hasn't done anything bad to me. Sure, she drugged me. And kidnapped me... adult-napped? But she feeds me. Provides for my basic needs. I get plenty of entertainment from the sheer amount of books she has. And the sex. *Fuuuuuck* is it good.

I am getting a much needed vacation. Haven't had one of those in the ten years I've had the shop. If Jamie gets in trouble, he can always call on Dad, it was his place before retirement. And I did kind of ask for it. I mean, I went to that bookstore to see if the social media shit was true. Was supposed to meet the guys there and make some kind of plan to catch ourselves book girls. And one caught me. I think I might be suffering from Stockholm's.

Yup, pretty sure I am.

I know she can hear me on the cameras but I don't know if she has something set up in her room, or is even awake. I don't want to alert her by talking. The clock on my screen says it is a few minutes after midnight. At dinner, she mentioned she had to work and now a stop at the grocery store.

Thumbing into the group message, I let them know what is going on. Someone is always awake. I should have probably waited until then to contact someone but I didn't think of that until just now.

BEEN DRUGGED
HELD HOSTAGE BY THE GIRL THAT WORKS THE BOOKSTORE

WES
So it is true!!!

JERYL
Is it like those videos?
Is she freaky?
Who is doing who?
Wait are you into butt stuff?

Of course it is these two that are still awake. Whether Wes is on shift or not, he stays up to not mess up his sleep schedule. Jeryl is probably neck deep in a stream of his latest game obsession. I can't knock it as he makes bank doing it.

I'm serious

WES
So are we
Your living the dream

JERYL
Living every mans dream
Are you tied up?
Ball gag?
Butt plug?

WES
Details!!

I'm fucking serious
She has to work tomorrow
Come get me when I call

I drop a pin in my location.

JERYL
Nope
Sorry bro

WES

YEAH

GOT TO TAKE ONE FOR THE TEAM

I'm about to bring down whatever hell fire I can rain on them. Plotting erasing Jeryl's whole gaming system. Hiding Wes's bike so he has to take the POS Festiva that makes him look like a clown getting out of that tiny ass thing his grandma left him. Three dots tell me my brother is awake and about to join in the conversation.

JAMIE

WHAT ARE U COMPLAINING ABOUT?

UNLESS IT IS LIKE THE MOVIE TOM CATS?

IS SHE SECRETLY A DOMME?

IS THERE A GRANNY?

ARE YOU FUCKING KIDDING ME?

YOUR MY BROTHER!

I DIDN'T SIGN UP FOR THIS

COME GET ME OR I WILL TELL MOM

I'm greeted with laughing faces and gifs. Hal L tells me snitches get stitches. Kitty Foreman, who looks a whole lot like our mom, laughs at me. Kermit is tied up and yelling.

JAMIE

GO AHEAD

I CAN'T WAIT TO HEAR U EXPLAIN THIS ONE

LIKE THAT TIME SHE FOUND YOUR PORNO COLLECTION

JERYL

YES!!!!!

I VOTE WE TELL MOM

JAMIE

BETTER YET WE WILL TELL DAD

Sighing, I resist chucking my phone across the room. My parents took them all in like they were those birds that get tricked into raising another bird's babies. It is times like this that I want to disown them all. And without a doubt, they would tell Mom and Dad everything. Deep breath as I attempt to calm down enough to think of a way to get these idiots to take this seriously. And why the fuck haven't they wondered where I am?

WHAT ABOUT WORK?

WHAT ABOUT WHEN PEOPLE NOTICE I'M MISSING?

MOM IS GOING TO WONDER WHERE I AM WHEN I DON'T SHOW FOR SUNDAY DINNER?

JAMIE
EYE ROLL EMOJI
YOU OWN WHERE YOU WORK
AND I'VE GOT IT COVERED
THIS SHIT ISN'T HARD
BOOK CAR IN, FIX CAR, BILL OWNER, SEND CAR OUT
AND I'LL JUST TELL PEOPLE YOU ARE SICK
OR OUT OF TOWN

I nearly sat up at that. Jamie is running the shop? Sure, he works there, but to run it? Don't get me wrong, he is a damn good mechanic but all the other bullshit that goes with it, he could care less about.

JERYL
DO YOU GET YOUR TOOLS FROM THE SNAP ON GUY?

More laughing emojis. A pulsing gif of something thick in a hole of something snap on pops up.

WES
OUT OF TOWN
IF YOU SAY SICK, MOM WILL WANT TO CHECK ON HIM

JAMIE
THUMBS UP

WHERE ARE YOU GOING TO TELL HER I AM?

WES
CONVENTION?

JERYL
VACATION?

Watching these idiots plan out the alibi to my kidnapping is agony.

JAMIE
NOPE
BUDDY NEEDING HELP DUE TO ACCIDENT
SPONTANEOUS AND LONG TERM

I need to get them back to them to the part of wondering where I am. Maybe it will encourage them to take this seriously and come get my ass.

DID ANY OF YOU NOT CARE WHERE I WAS?
THERE IS MORE TO IT THAN THAT
I'M GONNA CALL DAD

I swear I can hear the laughter with everything they send me at that. Thumbs moved before I could think better about that last part.

JAMIE
HE WILL TELL U TO SUCK IT UP
AND TAKE ONE FOR THE TEAM
AND I'LL TELL HIM IT WAS YOUR IDEA

WES
KIND OF FIGURED YOU MIGHT HAVE MET A CHICK
JUST LIKE THE VIDEOS SHOW

AND I'M GONE THIS LONG?

JERYL
HE DID!
AND SHE TOOK HIM DOWN!
ROFL EMOJI

WES
YOU HAVE BEEN KIND OF PENT UP
COULD HAVE FORGOT HOW IT ALL WORKED

JAMIE
BE A GOOD BOY AND EAT THAT PUSSY
HELL OF A WAY TO GO
NEVER CAN HAVE TO MUCH LUBE
RULE 34

Fucking little brothers. A middle finger emoji, as big as I can make it, fills the screen. Powering off the device, I slip it under the couch.

PLOT
TWIST
BABE

Ruby

Morning brings my alarm blaring a random song. This morning's pick, *Heat Of The Moment*. If it was Tuesday, I'd be worried. Slapping Asia silent, I sit up from the strange position I fell asleep in thanks to watching Tucker message someone, stretching muscles that have no business being this cramped first thing in the morning. My money is on the group of guys I gave pick up tips to. Especially since cops aren't knocking down my door.

Shuffling to the bathroom, I listen for a moment to make sure I don't walk in on a private moment I'm not ready to share with the man that is my unwilling guest. Unless he is pooping, he isn't in there making noise.

Braving the possibility that I might see, or smell, his morning routine, I turn the knob. Empty. Darting to the other door, I peek in.

Sprawled on the floor, half off the sleep pad, Tucker snores softly. He only does that when he sleeps on his back I've noticed. I need to get that phone back. And figure out how to get it unlocked. His screen was too smudged to figure it out when I took it off him.

Gently closing the door so as not to wake him, I sigh as I pee. First thing in the morning and after having to hold it a long time it happens involuntarily. Being able to go after both those instances will have me breathing in relief, and giving a little shiver when done. Kind of like when guys shake it off.

Wrinkling my nose at the thought of flicked drops, looking around like I might be able to see them, I finish and wash my hands. Teeth and face next. Head flipped over, I'm gathering my hair into my normal messy poufy knot when the knob rattles. Snapping the band from my wrist to the ball of fluff that is my look for the shop, the door opens on a sleep rumpled Tucker.

Not waiting for me to vacate, he moves to stand in front of the toilet. One hand on the wall above it, the other holding the elastic waist down with the space between ring and pinkie, pointing his half hard dick with his thumb and first finger. Slapping a hand over my eyes, I make a noise like a sick squeaky toy.

"Nope. Get over it. I'm tied to your shelf and you were taking too long. I heard you pissing anyway, so we are even." Tucker doesn't look at me while delivering that message of no privacy for bodily functions. Just yawns big, giving his own shiver before flicking the tip.

Ewww. Why can't men wipe?

Trying not to think of the things I've cleaned up at work in the men's room, I tighten the sash on my robe. "Breakfast?"

Mask pulled up over the bottom of his face, toothbrush tucked in his jaw, Tucker is looking at the scruff on his cheeks. "Got any yogurt? Egg whites?"

"Razors under the sink. Foam in the shower. Hope you don't mind lavender." Eyes meet mine in the mirror as he resumes brushing. "I'll pick up some stuff at the store. I'm having french toast but I can make you some regular toast."

"Got syrup?"

He ate five pieces. I brought up a stack of steaming egg soaked fried bread and he ate nearly all of it. Drenched in the maple syrup I picked up from the little farm stand down the road. Stopping the thigh clench as he licked the sticky drops from his fingers was impossible.

When my hand hits something just under the edge of the couch as I brace to stand, we both pause. Me in an awkward half lifted pose, him with his mug at his lips for that last sip of coffee.

Pulling his phone out, I tap the screen with my thumb. Off. Arching a brow, I hold it out to him. Might as well ask instead of locking us both out of the damn thing and getting caught trying to snoop. "Password?"

I'm sure the look of surprise on my face has me looking like a goldfish when he rattles it off. "9KM 5G7."

His plate number. Should have tried that one when I was in the garage trying variations of his make and model. Screen on, password in, I look at his recents. No phone calls. Figured that since I didn't hear him talking. Last texts were to a group called WHEEL NUTZ. Cute. Could have been worse.

Rolling back no farther than last night's time stamp, I read over the conversation. Snorting at the butt jokes. Tom Cats? I will have to look that one up. Giggling at the last thing his brother sent, I power it back off. "Well, now I have to look up whatever rule thirty-four is. Please tell me I won't be scared for life?"

"Just don't add anything to it. Jamie showed it to me with the word meatball and I can't unsee that shit now."

Tucker

Clacking keys wakes me. Ruby left lunch but stopped in to drop off the groceries and dinner. She was asked to cover closing and they had had a book launch party, needing extra hands with everyone that showed.

It was around ten that I decided to go to bed when I smacked myself in the face several times, dozing off while reading a big ass hardback I found on the shelf. *The Light Bearer* is nothing like the other books on the shelf and its Spartacus-esque theme has me diving in. The last thing I read for pleasure was the Goosebumps series in middle school. Miss Gillespie spins a great tale.

The room is lit by the soft glow of the little fireplace next to me. I can hear rain on the window behind my head, little rumbles of thunder add to the scene in front of me.

Lit by her monitors, I watch as Ruby works on something in front of her, attention darting to the right when she uses the second to help with her work on the left. A set of headphones with horns fixed to the band catches the blue light, making her look like a creature from another realm. Glasses keep me from seeing her eyes, adding to the theme of not being human.

My dick is doing the thinking as I pray she can't hear the chain with her ears covered. I crawl towards where she sits. If she is keeping me for sex, call me the more than willing participant. Face pinched not in thought but more in aggravation, I set about giving her some stress relief.

She doesn't flinch at the sound of the clinking chain following me, I rise to my feet behind her chair. One of the screens is spreadsheets and numbers that make no sense to me other than the fact that she must be working on the books for a business.

Grabbing the back of the chair, I wait for her to pause to check something on the papers to her far left before spinning it to face me. She jumps, giving a little scream. Big eyes look up at me as she grips her armrests. I can't help the smirk on my face at having surprised her.

She pushes something on the headset before cocking her head at me curiously. Taking the glasses, I lay them behind her. Feeding into the fantasy in my head, I leave the horns. Holding out my hands, I pull her to her feet, stepping around her so we are front to back. Taking her wrists, I use my body to push her to the wall.

Nose running up her neck into her hair, I breathe in the scent of coffee, sugar, and something that is pure Ruby. The mask does nothing to mute her, imprinting it deeper into my soul. With a nip to the place below her ear, I give her wrists a firm press. "Don't move your hands."

The thin straps of her tank are no opposition for me. Snapping them, I push it down her body. Breasts uncovered, I can't help the squeeze and heft I give them. My long fingers do more than play piano and guitar. They are just the right length for wrapping those lush mounds, molding the pliant flesh, squeezing.

Returning to the task, I push what is left of her tank down her stomach, hooking the waist of the little pair of shorts she is wearing with it, dragging it all down to her ankles. Her toes are painted in contrast to the dark nails on her fingers in white. A silver ring winks at me in the blue glow from the middle toe of her left foot.

Pressing so the skin divots, I trace back up her legs with a firm touch. That ass in front of my face flexes as she rises to her toes. Sinking my teeth into the cheek in front of me, I am rewarded with a squeak and the taste of the laundry soap I use since I forgot to pull up the bottom of my balaclava.

Jerking it up, clear to my forehead, I wrap my fingers over her hip bones, angling them back, bowing her from the wall. "Step out. Let me in."

She only pauses for a second, either in thought or due to the hitch I can hear in her voice telling me she is turned on. Once there is room, I dive in. Lapping at her wet pussy, sucking her clit the best I can from this position. Plunging two fingers into her wet channel, I hold them still as she attempts to ride them.

Now I got her distracted trying to reach her own pleasure, I move back. Free hand parting those trembling cheeks, I lick right across where my fingers are holding steady to the puckered hole that is flexing with her hips.

That squeak was higher in pitch. With an evil grin, I dive in. Pressing with my tongue, gets her hips pulled away so I stick to firm licks. Wet to my wrist from how turned on she is, I slurp it all up.

Standing, I let my thumb take the place of my tongue, pressing my back to hers. Hand planted on the wall next to hers. "Such a good girl." I know she can hear me with the shudder of breath that escapes her. "Now, come for me."

I dropped the hand that was on the wall to her clit. Moving the fingers she was trying to ride in a harsh rhythm, Ruby comes with a cry, pressing her face and chest to the wall to help hold her up. But I would never let her fall.

Hands on her hips, I guide her back as I sit in her chair. Cock so hard I don't have to hold it up as I slide into her welcome heat. Legs on either side of mine, I lean back in the leather with a groan of my own.

Spreading her as far as I can, I pinch her clit before rubbing it the way that she likes, "ride it. Make me cum for you."

Hands on my knees, toes barely touching the floor, Ruby does as she is told. She doesn't get much lift, her pulsing pussy clamped down so tight on me I grit my teeth. Working her clit, I pinch it between my fingers, pressing into the wet flesh on either side of it as it slides in my grip with her movements.

"I'm going to cum!" Breathy moans and gasps flee those parted lips as her head lands on my shoulder.

"Hold it."

Whines are my answer as I torture us both just a little longer to see if she can follow my commands.

"Please, please, *please, PLEASE.*" The noises she draws from me belong to an animal more than the man seated under her.

"Cum. Cum for me."

I barely say the first word before her pussy is clenching on me. I follow with a shout. Pulsing into the hot depths of her.

Panting, I chuckle. This is definitely a well made chair. "That was wild."

Ruby nods to the shelves of the books I've been looking at, some marked so finding the spicy parts are easy, "you've read worse."

"Can I keep you?" Shit. The words are out before I can think about them. Jerking my mask down as she sits up, I can do nothing but wait to see what she does.

Ruby stands, kisses me over the mask as she reaches around to turn her computer off. The headphones she sets on my head muffles her response as she walks away, naked with my cum running down her thighs. "Plot twist, you're mine to keep until you figure it out."

MAYBE THIS AIN'T DEFEAT

Tucker

I'm dreaming. I know I am. But I can feel the air. Feel the cool caress of fall as it seeps into my suit. Down my back, across my chest.

Shifting gears I take the turn in front of me faster than I should, nearly needing to set my knee to pavement. Open road in front of me. Trees in fall dress blur by in a kaleidoscope of colors.

I can smell it. Damp earth as it prepares to sleep for a season. Wet leaves as they attempt to cling just a little longer to their trees. Smoke from fires to warm and soothe.

Tinting on my visor shifts the tones around me into something deeper. Bright orange, yellow, red are given a slight grey tint. My visor self tints and has the bright flicker of sun through trees toned down. Yellow center lines are just a suggestion to where I ride.

Another gear and my bike whines as it speeds up faster. This is the only time my brain quiets. Sounds of responsibility and family and friends all fade. Life just pauses as speed takes me to a place that I can just be.

That is a lie.

Well, not the truth now.

I have another happy place.

Scents of ink and paper replace the leaves. Fresh air is toasted coffee with fall spice. Warmth of a home that I am starting to feel comfortable in replaces the chill in my chest.

The road turns again and there is the café. Warm light beckons from inside. Windows wink at me, knowing that they hold the answers I've been looking for. I'm off my bike and walking inside before I remember parking.

But it is a dream and things are more fluid here. Instead of the smell of coffee and printed words I arrive in the room that has been my home for the last week. Vanilla and dark cherry with spice. Has it been a week? That doesn't matter as Ruby walks up to me in a tee shirt I recognize as my own from the oil stain on the sleeve.

My shop logo stretches over her tits. One shoulder droops down her arm. Her hips push at the fabric making me want to sink my fingers into that supple flesh. The heather blue makes her eyes seem deeper. Hair in that messy knot that I want to use to steer her to her knees before ripping her bare and devouring all she has to offer. Sinking into wet heat that fits me perfectly.

"Can I keep you?" That rasp she has settles right in the center of my chest with her question.

Isn't that my line? I mean it was Casper's and he was a guy when he asked that chick the same thing.

I open my mouth to tell her yes. Promise forever.

Jeff Healey croons out about the Angel Eyes of his woman, startling me awake.

Rubbing my hands down my face, I realize I pulled my cover off again. Ruby's rule to keep my face covered is strange but

I figure she wants me to have a way to avoid her should we ever meet again once I go home.

Huh. That realization hurt a little. Flipping my bedding, I find the black piece of cloth and pull it back on. Standing there with my ankle strapped in a way that is now familiar instead of alien, I analyze that little twinge.

Do I want to go home?

I can't just abandon the shop. Dad, and his before him, spilled blood, sweat, and tears to make it what it is. I put myself into so much debt modernizing it so we could build custom sportbikes while still sticking to our roots. My own time, effort, and life is painted in that cinderblock and cement building.

Sure Dad could un-retire. Probably would with the amount of time he spends in the place still. Mom might kill me herself though. Jamie could use with learning the ropes so that I can have some more freedom. But dammit, the place is mine and I'm fucking proud of that.

And the guys. Wes and Jeryl, Happy and KC, Jonsey and Chad. All are younger than me. I'm kind of the default leader. Keeping them out of trouble. Those three in morning calls have come enough over the years that I am reaching for clothes and shoes before even answering the phone.

I got Wes his job when he couldn't find something that played into that fancy art degree he got. Gave him and Jeryl the apartment over the garage when Jeryl got them thrown out of their last place for his all night gaming. Happy and KC owe me so much in bike repairs. Chad was there for my last break up and I am there for *all* his. And Jonsey. He works for me. I paid for his schooling when he got out of jail when no one else would give Jamie's best friend a second chance.

Jamie. Fucking little brothers. And he is mine and I'm proud of that. Kid did some stupid shit in high school with his best friend. Nearly got himself killed. But I was the one that gave him a place in the crew. Taught him to ride. How to work on the bikes.

The answer to that is yes.

I want to go home.

The dream world was telling the truth.

I feel at peace here. The warmth of these walls has called to something in me that I didn't know was missing. And Ruby.

Fucking hell. That woman drugs me. Kidnaps me. Asks nothing of me.

I have this feeling that if I had asked, insisted, she would have let me go. Sure, I thought she wanted something sexual out of this but she never made a move. That was all me. And me each time after. And what a move it was.

I palm my hard dick as humming signals she is on the move to the kitchen to make breakfast.

But then again, no.

I don't want to go.

BEG FOR ME

Ruby

Pulling a double gets me the next day off. I'll have to finish the books for the quarter before I was interrupted last night. But damn, was it a hell of a way to get my brain to stop screaming at me it was too tired to do that kind of work.

Humming to the song that woke me this morning, I begin my morning with making some fancy coffee. I normally just pop a pod in the machine in the corner but not today. Something about multiple orgasms has me indulging. I pull the cover off the fancy machine that takes up more counterspace than I can spare.

Setting two perfect lattes on the tray, I set it in the dumbwaiter and press the second floor button. I love my house. It was nearly falling down when I bought it.

Inspectors and contractors alike told me it was a lost cause. But I fell in love with the character. With the vibe she had. Sad she had been neglected, I felt her perk up when I walked in. Three years of little sleep. Hundreds, if not thousands, of YouTube videos. More money than I want to think about. But here we are.

Wood shiny again. Floors restored. Character enhanced with my dark academia vibe. Life breathed back into her. And me.

Balancing the tray on my arm, I enter the code to a door that I normally keep open. Even if he is fastened with a very thick chain, I can't tempt Tucker with an open door. That would be just cruel.

I can hear the water running in the bathroom since the door can't shut with his leash in it. I focus on setting out breakfast over trying to get a peek at him. Egg white omelet with whole wheat toast and turkey sausage for him. My bowl of multi-colored round balls drips milk I wipe up with my napkin. Crunching on the kids' cereal, I hum as I look over at the game plan for today.

One of the real gems of this house is on the first floor. Every book girl dreams of owning a library. Shelves from floor to ceiling with one of those rolling ladders is off the right of the foyer. This room is for my purposes.

These shelves are for my personal annotated books and my own work. I've removed everything for the work needing finished. My OCD and anxiety are screaming at me that my books and keepsakes are not where they need to be. If I don't finish this soon, it is going to drive me crazy.

Another job that was happily interrupted. I need to remove the rest of the shelves. Bring up the timbers I sanded to a satin finish. Anchor them in which means going into the servants passageway behind the wall to do that. What I'm installing needs to be sturdy, safe.

Tucker comes out, a towel slung around his hips. Water clings to his skin. Drops trailing down to be absorbed in the terry cloth. I have to restrain myself from jumping to my feet and licking them off him. Down the chain are his wadded up pants since he can't get them off with the cuff locked to his ankle. I'll get him new clothes this evening.

"Morning." Setting the remaining milk and bowl aside, I wait for Tucker to come see what I made for him. I'm no Suzy

Homemaker but I do take care of my guests. And my love language is acts of service.

Mug in my hands, I smile at his hum of approval. Setting on his cushion, he digs in after moving the bottom of the mask up. Nodding, he takes a drink from his own cup. "This is good. Thank you."

I preen at the praise. What this man does to me with those little words.

Tucker

I watch as Ruby comes in with those coveralls and toolbelt again. If she was paying attention to me and not what she was doing, she'd see exactly what that outfit does to me as pajama pants will not hide it.

"What are you building?" Maybe I should have asked that the day she almost brained herself, but we did get distracted.

Muscles I didn't know she had flex as the huge piece of wood is fit into place diagonally. She tosses me a smirk over her shoulder while holding the beam in place with her body and digging into her belt pocket for a length of metal nearly as long as my forearm she threads into a predrilled hole. Stepping back, she holds her hands out to catch it in case it shifts. Nodding when it stays, she goes over to the little frog and opens the hidden door. With a raised brow to rival the ones I throw at her, "don't get any ideas."

With a snort, I watch the board shake and give a slide as if to fall to the floor. Darting up, I shove it back into place. I can hear a clicking noise from the other side of the wall. Knowing the sound of a ratchet, I wait until the clicking slows before releasing and giving it a testing shake. Sturdy.

Stepping back I take in the board. There is another hole the same distance from the top in the bottom for another bolt. In the center is a groove with a square section left the thickness for something to be fit over it and two more recessed bolt holes. Half way down from the tip on the right and equal distance down from the middle on the left are two thick pegs. The whole thing is smooth and stained to match the shelves behind it.

I jump when I turn to sit back down, finding Ruby standing next to me. "Figure it out yet?"

Pure evil joy is the only way to describe the look she gives me. "Nope. But even if it means I'm more than likely going to end up tied to it, I'll help you so you don't get hurt or break something."

With a nod, Ruby turns to the room door she left open when she brought the piece in. "I'll be right back then."

A fuck and a thumping scrape reaches my ears, followed shortly by Ruby carrying in the second part. Grunting and instructions that remind me of my dad telling me to hold the light when helping him as a kid has it slide into place. All bolts threaded in and me holding this one as she moved behind the wall.

Stepping back as far as my arms will allow, I see it is a mirror image for the pegs when I get what it is.

HOLY SHIT!!

Ruby built a saint andrew's cross.

A hand on my bicep guides me back to where she stands in the center of the room to look over her creation. If you know where to look, you can see the older shelves hiding the door she added to. Those new shelves are now framed by thick timbers waiting for a victim.

Ruby

I leave Tucker to look over my newest piece of furniture. The shower is beckoning me. Stripping down, I sigh as the heat washes the sweat off. Tilting my head back and then to each side. Rolling shoulders. Pressing my hands to my lower back I arch. That bitch was heavy and I now have a hole in my drywall coming up the stairs.

"I know this is a dumb question, but what is that for?"

Wiping the steam from the shower door finds Tucker standing in the middle of the room with his legs spread, arms crossed. I kind of wish there wasn't a mask rule. But when he escapes, he needs to be able to pretend he doesn't know me when we cross paths again, should we ever. A hum is the only answer I give him as I rinse the soap from my back before turning off the spigot.

"You think I'm going to willingly let you strap me to that thing, you got another think coming."

He doesn't move as I dry off and wrap the towel around myself. A smirk is the only answer I give him as I go into my room for something to wear the rest of the evening. A large stretched tee and tiny pair of shorts is on the corner of my bed where I left them.

"Woman."

That has me laughing as I turn now I'm dressed and stand to copy him, my arms plumping my breasts up and catching his attention. "I think you will. Be more than willing, that is."

SHELVED & CUSTOM MADE

Tucker

I'm tied to the fucking cross.

After a long talk about consent and safe words, Ruby produced a set of keys from her nightstand, the happy jingle of them must have gone to my head. Not being tied to her tropes clouded my thinking. Maybe if I keep telling myself that, I'll believe that is what got me here. Not the idea of being at her mercy, which I already am. But complete and utterly a slave to her whims.

Looking up at the cuffs around my wrists, I give them a test. They are the same as the one that resides normally around my ankle just without the loop for a lock. These have a strip of velcro as wide as my wrist. I'm not getting out of them without help. I know, I've tried to get the one off my ankle on many occasions. She explained that they were neoprene like deep diving suits are made out of. These are made for weight and resistance training. The strain they will take, and I've put the one she keeps me tethered with to the test, so I should know.

I had watched as that ass bounced and jiggled as she screwed eye bolts into lined holes I hadn't noticed before clipping on short chains with straps dangling from them.

Straps now wrapping my naked limbs, keeping me spread eagle.

Fuck.

Damn Jeryl and his talk of butt stuff.

"Um," I raise my voice to where Ruby disappeared back into her room after stringing me up, "I'm not into butt stuff. I mean, I've had a finger up there from an ex who was a nurse. Not gonna lie, it was a fucking awesome experience cumming that hard and fast, but I'm not into *other* things up there."

"That is good to know." I can hear the laughter in her voice.

Steps sound on the bathroom tiles telling me she is coming for me.

Can you swallow your tongue?

Stopping in the middle of the room, she waits for me to take all of her in. Hand on a cocked hip, she gives that little smirk that makes me want to spank her ass and kiss her at the same time. My adam's apple bobs with my dry swallow, hard.

"Tom Cats. The librarian." Words rasp out of me from how dry my mouth is.

"After your little convo with your friends, I rented that. It was pretty funny. She was my favorite character. Are you a doodler? Do you break spines? Dogear pages?"

"Please don't have a granny waiting behind a door."

Head back in a laugh, her hair hangs in a tangle of just fucked looking curls she gets when she takes it out of that messy bun she likes. I want to grab it, drag her to me. She didn't do purple. No, Ruby would only do something that fits her name.

A deep red corset tightly wraps around her body. Breasts pushed up and barely held back. I swear I can see her nipples peeking out. I would expect a thong but why wear something skimpy when you can wrap your ass in a red lace that looks like it was painted on? Without asking, she gives a little turn. The back has this heart shaped cut out letting me see butt cleavage. To finish off the outfit, she has on these black boots to her knees. I can see some kind of tall sock or whatever women wear that is see through bunched at the top of them. Laces, buckles, and platform thick soles.

The only thing that would make this better was a helmet. She needs a helmet. I want to get her a helmet. Install my backpack seat and drop those pegs that no one has ever ridden on. She needs to be on the back of my bike, arms wrapped around me. Hot core pressing into me as the vibrations mimic the vibrator I'm sure is in her bedside drawer.

Hands sliding up my chest draw me from images of her on the back of my bike. Bent over my bike. In front of me on my bike as I fuck her. "No granny. Just you and me."

Denim blue eyes look up from where she slides to her knees between my spread feet. I'm hard and dripping. There is probably a wet spot on the carpet from the precum I've dribbled since she walked in the room.

Tongue out, she licks from the base to the head before enclosing it in those lips painted to match her outfit. That smirk comes out to play when she pops off me. And then...

FUCKING HELL!!!!

To the base. She just took all of me to the base. Her nose is pressed to my groin. She just swallowed! I can't. She has to stop. All I can do is repeat fuck, over and over. Pulling back, she sucks back to the tip, making that little pop sound again when she's done hoovering my cock. I thicken, balls drawing up, I can feel that throb that says I'm cumming.

She stops.

And so does my brain.

What just happened? Ruby has her fingers wrapped around the base of my cock in a tight grip and is gently pulling my sack back down. The urge to cum fades. The tunnel expands to the room and not just the goddess at my feet.

"Ready?"

I was more than ready. Before I can answer her, she steps back. The rasp of a zipper is loud in the silence that was only broken by my panting breaths as my soul was preparing to evacuate. The front of the corset gaps open exposing creamy silk skin with nipples hard enough to cut glass. Letting it fall to the floor, Ruby hooks her thumbs into the waist of her panties. With that little hip wiggle that makes my dick jump, she pushes them down.

With a look of complete concentration and maybe a little prayer that the assembled cross holds us both, she reaches for the hand holds. Eyes on mine, she steps high, planting one boot and then the other. Hot pussy connects with my aching cock.

With a breath that sounds a little like she is bracing herself for things to go wrong, she lets go with one hand and lines me up. Wet folds part as she rubs the head at her entrance. It is then I feel something forward on her clit. "What...?"

Her cheeks go a little pink. The woman who wants to write our sexcapades, kidnapped me, has me strapped to a fucking saint andrew's cross, is embarrassed?

Leaning forward, I press a kiss into her lips. It must work to reassure her even if I can't deepen it with my hands out of commission.

"I have a Lush in. It, um…" Her voice trails off and the pink deepens on her cheeks.

"Look, I've got no problems with toys in the bedroom. Team effort and all that as long as everyone gets off. They are especially helpful if you work with your hands like I do and they are sore but you want to play with your girl or yourself. Whatever floats your boat."

Nodding, she finishes what she was going to say, "it is a g-spot vibe with a little part outside the body. I set it up to run nonstop in a pre-programed pattern. I didn't think there would be a whole lot of help from either of us to 'get me there' with the cross."

I heard the air quotes even if she wasn't able to do the finger action of them. "So it is inside you," she nods, "and I'll fit with it?" She nods again. "And it is vibrating right now?" Another nod, "and it is going to vibrate on me too?"

That final nod has me throwing back my head, it knocks into the shelf of books behind the giant X bolted to them. "I'm not going to make it out of this alive."

Ruby gives a little snort laugh.

"Ok, hop up here and let's give this a go. No promises I'm going to last long."

Ruby's hand returns to the peg on my left as she sinks down on my dick. I can feel the toy as her body gives to make room for us both. She was snug to begin with but this is strangling my cock. And the vibrations.

"Are they getting stronger?"

Ruby nods, biting her lip as the hum inside her body steadily builds from whatever she did to that toy. Arms and thighs tense, she moves to ride me. Moans and gasps fill the air as she works herself on me. The slide of her wet channel up and down my dick has me quoting bike stats to keep from blowing too soon. If I had her pressed to a wall, holding her up and in place, this is how it would work. But I'm the one pressed into an upright surface, being fucked and I am here for it.

"Ruby! Is it..."

My shout has my ears ringing as the vibrations hit some kind of peak and we both go off. Her pussy is gripping me in pulsing waves as her muscles contract. One foot slips, signaling the shaking in her limbs is going to make her fall. I can't do a damn thing about it as my own are just as jiggly and still tethered.

"Ruby? Love? Can you get down? Let me loose? We need to be laying down after all that."

Boots drag across my thighs as she maneuvers off the foot pegs. Holding on with her left hand, she grabs the cuff on my wrist and rips the velcro open before letting go and collapsing onto the carpet. I fumble with my restraints before joining her.

Pulling her into my side, I press our sweat sticky skin together and a kiss to her head.

A VILLAIN, A LIBRARIAN, TENSION, & WARFARE

Ruby

One of my favorite things about the bookshop is when authors come. It doesn't matter if they are trad or indie. Nervous or excited. I love the vibe when you are in an area filled with those that love books. The normal smells of ink and paper with the coffee and sweets get this layer of anticipation woven into it that just enhances the whole mood.

I don't have to work this one like I normally do, so I'm dressed in what I call my normie clothes. I turn in the mirror to make sure that the skirt I picked enhances my butt instead of making it into a bubble on my pear shaped form. The cropped burnt orange tee shows the slight curve I have to my belly and the couple of inches it doesn't cover between it and the waistband of the black crepe material that swishes around my ankles. Over this I have a cardigan I crocheted myself out of skull centered granny squares.

Flicking the black glasses chain back over my head, I settle it on the outside of my collar to make sure it doesn't tangle with the trio of long necklaces and crystals I am wearing to get my extroverted ass through this. If I had my way, I'd stay home and write. But money doesn't grow on trees and a girl has to eat. Every day I layer on my protections to get me to and from work and errands. Even something I enjoy, like this signing, has to be prepped well in advance. Mentally, physically, spiritually.

As I sit on the end of my bed to tie up my ankle height converses, Tucker stops as far as the chain will let him go in the bathroom in front of my bedroom door. "Is this really necessary?"

I look up from tucking the laces into the inner sides of the shoes to see him pointing to the ankle cuff. "I'm going out. I don't think you have gained enough trust for me to leave it off you when I don't know how long I'll be gone. Freedom is earned with trust if you remember and the first chance you got it, you took a tour of the inside of my walls."

Arms cross over the new tee I gave him last night after our fun on the saint andrew's. The pajama pants are a little short since I have a penchant to shrink things. "Let's talk about trust. Do you know how much trust it took for me to let you tie me to that thing? To use me. How about the fact I had my phone? Could have called the police and didn't? Refused to sign that paper letting you tell people about the shit we do."

A twinge of hurt has me lashing back at him. "That is different. This is different."

He huffs out a breath through his nose, "no, it isn't. Trust is trust."

Still wondering where the idea that him calling what we did no more than me tying him to 'that thing' hurts. So does the 'shit we do' comment. I don't answer, so he goes on.

"You have me locked in that room. I'm sure you fixed the secret door so I can't get out of it. And the window is sealed in some way. Short of breaking it, risking cutting myself to pieces, and breaking something when I jump from the second floor, there is no way I can get out."

He has a point. He trusted me with his body. I need to trust him with my heart. But that is just it. If he leaves, a piece of me goes with him. And I don't think it will be okay this time. Something about all this is different.

"Take the fucking lock off, Ruby." The growl in his tone has me looking up at him from where I was looking at the floor, wringing my hands.

With a shake of my head, I shut the door between him and my bedroom, locking it. Tucker shouts my name, the chain dragging on the tiles as he moves from the bathroom to the office. Pounding on that door follows me down the hallway.

I can't. I can't take it off. What if he leaves me?

His anger is so loud that it only silences when I shut the car door. Looking up at the house, I see him silhouetted in the window. The glass does nothing to temper the glare aimed my way. "I'm sorry."

I know he can't hear me but he turns away after I say it.

Putting our argument out of my head is harder than it should be. Even if I'm not working tonight, I'm expected to be here having set it up. Pasting on a smile, I walk into the reading. Greeting several of the locals that come to every one, no matter who it is we are hosting. I pick up my copy and wait in line for the author to autograph it.

Turning to find my own seat, I nearly jumped out of my skin to see two of the crew that showed up looking for Tucker. I know they know. But do they know it is me? There are three other females that work here, it could really be any of us.

Taking my seat, I wait to see what they will do. Flirting. Lots and lots of flirting. Seems they took the advice I gave them and are running with it. I see the Mister Shego get the number of two women waiting to get their books signed and the other one gets the author's no less.

As they sit behind me, I attempt to remain calm.

Both of their phones go off just as Natasha steps up to make her intro and the request to silence devices.

Mister Shego gives a muffled snort as the tone slowly silences. "Tuck got his phone back."

"Really? What's he want now? Still want to leave?"

"Daaammmn. Look at that."

"Is that a...X built into the bookshelves? With restraints?"

I fight the urge to turn and snatch the phone from his hands.

Tucker

As her car backs out of the driveway, I turn and look at the room around me. The sudden urge to reduce it to rubble is so foreign to me, I literally stagger back. I would never do that to Ruby. I have watched her sit there and write about us several nights. To do that to her would be heartbreaking. Almost as heartbreaking as when she walked in here and locked that cuff back while I was reading.

I had sat there staring at it for so long, she was ready to leave before I snapped out of it. I didn't even ask where she was going or when she would return. I just got mad. She didn't reattach it to me after riding me to a spectacular finish. Just smiled after wishing me good night and shutting her bedroom door.

The idea to leave was nowhere near the forefront of my brain. It had felt different. We had felt different. My only complaint was that I hadn't been able to sleep with her. I would have loved to hold her all night. To wake with her this morning. To help with breakfast. To kiss her goodbye when she left for work.

I understood that that was not how this worked. That I would be regulated to this room. But to have the chain dragging after me once again hurt.

Looking up at the cross, I took deep steadying breaths. Reaching up, I tweaked one of the dangling straps. Letting my brain run on auto pilot, I looped a finger in an eyebolt and gave it a twist. They were in tight, but it unscrewed and lay in my hand while my body did one thing and my heart screamed at the pain it was feeling.

The weight in my palm snapped me out of the fugue state I was in. Turning to the desk with my tool, I sat in Ruby's chair. Memories of what we did in that chair flickered to life, but I snuffed them as I placed the pointy end of the bolt against the seam where the drawer front met desk and smacked it with my other palm.

It took three more hits and more than likely a bruised hand from the impact, but I have had worse. My phone lay in there with the portable scanner just like before. Snatching it up, I powered it on. Twenty-three percent battery.

PICTURE OF CROSS

I didn't have to wait long before they all saw it.

JERYL
HOLY SHIT!!!

JAMIE
A FUCKING ST ANDREWS

WES
PLEASE TELL ME YOU LET HER TIE YOU UP TO THAT

KC
DUDE! HAPPY WANTS TO KNOW WHAT IT WAS LIKE BEING THE ONE CATCHING

JONESY
I BET SHE ROCKED HIS WORLD

THE CHAD
GIF OF A WHIP BEING SNAPPED

I wait for them to settle down before I answer as Chad sets off a string of innocent but now raunchy gifs.

SOMEONE COME GET ME

More denial and negatives fill the screen. It is Jamie who quiets them down.

JAMIE
WHY?

That one word has them all waiting to see what I say. And what do I say? My thoughts are all a jumble. The main sticking point is that she doesn't trust me. That she chained me back up. Sure, I need to go back to work. And my mom is probably missing me, wondering where I am. Dad won't care since there is really nothing wrong with me. He'd call it a forced vacation. The guys all think I'm living some fantasy.

I give the only answer I can.

IT IS TIME

More gifs follow that. Many with a monkey hitting a lion with a stick.

JAMIE
IF YOU ARE SERIOUS
I'LL COME GET U
BUT THE SHOP IS OK
MOM AND DAD ARE OK

JERYL
YOU HAVEN'T BEEN GONE 2 WEEKS

A PROPER VACATION IS AT LEAST 2
3 FOR A PENT UP PRICK LIKE YOU

It hasn't been two weeks? I sit back thinking it over. It was a Wednesday when I woke up here but then the days blur together. It feels like longer. These feelings should have taken longer to settle in. No way I have fallen for Ruby in less than two weeks.

Fuck. I've fallen for Ruby. I have feelings for the woman who abducted me and kept me chained in her home.

I THINK I'VE FALLEN FOR HER

They are my family so they have a right to know what is going on. Even if they have no intent on saving me.

HAPPY
AND THIS IS A PROBLEM HOW?

JERYL
STONEHENGE

WES
WHAT?

JERYL
YOU KNOW
THAT THING WHERE THEY FALL FOR THEIR KIDNAPPER
ADULT-NAPPER?

JAMIE
U MEAN STOCKHOLM YOU IDIOT

IT ISN'T THAT
I FEEL LIKE IF I REALLY ASKED SHE'D LET ME GO

I take a moment to think over telling them what happened. Would they get it? Fuck it. I need to tell someone and Dad isn't here. I'd clue him in, but he would tell Mom and she doesn't need to know this shit.

LAST NIGHT FELT DIFFERENT

THE CHAD
WELL THE FIRST TIME BEING A BOTTOM CAN DO THAT
DID SHE USE ENOUGH LUBE?

I have to wait for them to settle down again. I'm second guessing doing this when Jamie is the voice of authority again and I'm set to thinking that the pod people got my brother or having the responsibility of my shop might have given him the jolt he needed to grow up.

JAMIE
SHUT UP
HE IS TRYING TO EXPLAIN THIS SHIT
AND THAT IS MY FUTURE SISTER U ALL ARE TALKING ABOUT

What the fuck? That image strikes fire to a part of my brain that burns with ideas of introducing her to my parents. Proposing. A wedding. Riding off into the sunset on my bike. Kids. Shaking my head, I tap out the rest of what I was going to say.

I'VE BEEN TIED UP AND SHE DIDN'T AFTER WE HAD SEX
THEN SHE PUT IT BACK ON THIS EVENING AND LEFT
AND I DON'T KNOW, WE HAD A SORT OF FIGHT

JAMIE
DO U WANT ME TO COME GET YOU?

I look at the door and the locks I know are there. He could get in. Hell, he'd just bring a hammer and bash them off. Or a chainsaw and cut the doors down. The cross catches my attention again. And then the helmets on the opposite wall. Mine sitting there with the other two. The way she crumpled when she told me they didn't stay.

Did she drug them too? Or were they willing? I need to ask her about them. I need to know what the game plan is.

No

LACK OF COPING SKILLS

Ruby

Stopping in front of the garage, I take a moment to look over my house. I am a fall girlie. But when I picked the color for the exterior, I wanted something that would pop against all those shades of autumn. Cobalt blue won the vote. With the navy and cream accents, it is a pretty sight when the leaves change.

Wood siding and all those elegant trim pieces make it look like something from a bygone era. And she is. With those big windows and the huge front door with the knob in the center. The porch that calls out to you to sit a spell. I've dressed her for the season with pumpkins in every color and shape I could fit into the back of my car trickling down the steps.

Enough dawdling. Stepping out of the car, I sling my bag full of goodies from tonight over my shoulder. Reaching in to where the remote is sticky taped to the dash, I take a deep breath. Bracing for impact, I push the button for the garage door. The air whooshes out of me.

It is still here.

He is still here.

Sitting in the middle of my garage, Tucker's bike shines in the overhead lights that come on when the door opens. I walk around it twice to see if it has moved since I parked it here, taking up the space my own vehicle usually occupies. Glinting from the floor in front of the back tire, the penny I placed to monitor just for that winks at me.

With a smile that feels out of place with the riot in my belly at seeing him after we argued, I flick off the lights at the door to the house, letting myself into the dark kitchen.

Trudging up the stairs like I'm about to face a firing squad, I move to the door to the office. Palm on the wood, I listen for movement beyond. Nothing. He must be asleep. I'm quiet as I strip down in my bedroom, pulling on a large tee that advertises the café and how we like our books and coffee both steamy.

Using habit and the little light I keep plugged in next to the vanity in the bathroom, I remove my makeup and do my nightly routine. I'm just spitting the final time, rinsing my toothbrush, when the door behind me opens.

In the dim light his eyes look black. He isn't wearing his mask but the nightlight isn't reaching that door with me in front of it. Meeting mine in the mirror, we just stand watching each other. The shadows act like his mask and keep me from knowing if he is still angry. I know what I'm about to do is in no way an apology, but it needs doing. Picking up the cold metal key from the counter, I step in front of Tucker, eyes on our toes. Taking his hand where it hangs limply next to his side, I place it in his callused palm, closing his fingers over it.

He has two ways out of the room. The secret door. I only fixed the draft, not locking it like he thinks. Second, through my room. Where I will pretend to not see as he walks out. Pretend he isn't taking that part of me I gave him without his knowledge with him.

His other hand raises as if to touch me but I step back. Back in my room, I lean on the closed door, swallowing the sobs that want to break free. Cold sheets, cold pillows, empty bed are the altar I lay on in the judgement I have brought on myself.

Somewhere between sleep and that wakeful place, the door between Tucker and I opens. I don't look for fear that it is wishful thinking on my part.

Warmth slides into the bed behind me. Arms lean in muscle wrap me up, pulling me into the little spoon to his big one. He nuzzles into the back of my hair before kissing my shoulder followed by another where my neck joins it. "Tell me about the helmets."

I knew he was going to ask. I saw him looking at them on several occasions when I checked the cameras. He even took them down once, looking inside for a name possibly. His own sitting there untouched over the last few weeks.

"The red one belonged to who I thought was my fiancé. I met him in college." I swallow down the image of his smiling face, that tousled blond hair, eyes a brighter shade of blue than mine. "He was studying sports physiotherapy and nutrition. Was a baseball player and had a scholarship to play for the university. I was flattered when he approached me in the library one Saturday."

Tucker's arms tighten on me when he hears the self depreciation in my tone. He doesn't like it, but lets me go on without interruption. "Soon it was 'good morning beautiful' and 'I can't stop thinking of you' and 'when can I see you again' and 'I'll see you in my dreams'. Three years I walked around with my head in a cloud and my feet barely touching the ground. His ring on my finger just three months after we started seeing each other.

"I was coming home early from work at the coffee shop on campus. It was his birthday and I wanted to surprise him. The sound of a bike caught my attention when I would normally ignore it. Guess my subconscious knew it was his. On the back was his study partner. Her helmet matching his. When they stopped at the light, their hands were all over each other.

"I followed them. It wasn't far to the housing for the athletes from that light. His bike was parked in the usual spot. I let myself in with the key he had given me but never used. I could hear them. She sounded like a bad porno.

"I stood frozen to that spot just inside the door. When he walked out naked with her cum still on his cock, he hadn't used a condom with her but insisted on them with me. I just... He was walking towards me. Saying something but it sounded like the adults in those Charlie Brown comics. I grabbed the first thing I could lay my hands on. His helmet.

"The part that protects your chin," I felt him nod where his forehead was against the back of my head, "fit perfectly in my hand. I swung it. The sound it made when it connected with the side of his head was satisfying. I know it shouldn't have been. I know I should have just walked out. But seeing him stagger to the side. The blood running down the side of his face. I didn't even know I had his helmet until I was back in my dorm.

"Turns out so many people knew. I was some kind of joke. There were other girls too. She knew. His 'study buddy'. They were high school sweethearts. Their parents were best friends. It was expected of them to marry. Him being with me was just him getting it out of his system before the wedding. I found all that out over the next week. Finished my degree remotely. Didn't attend graduation."

Turning in Tucker's arms, I am glad for the dark so I don't see the same looks I get from people who know the story. My own parents have this pitying look they get when the subject of me being alone comes up. Brittany and others like her look like they stepped in something bad when my relationship status is questioned.

The limited light lets me see nothing but anger. Rearing back, trying to push from Tucker's embrace, I wonder what I did wrong. Is he still mad about being locked back up? Does he think it was all my fault? Or is this because I hit a biker bro?

"Ruby, stop."

I go still. I don't even breathe.

"His name." The air leaves me on a laugh. He may be mad but not at me. "His name, Ruby. In no world is cheating acceptable. But it could have been one and done. Instead he lied to you. Played a game that you didn't know the rules of. Now, tell me his name."

Shaking my head, I nestle into the solid chest in front of me. Pushing until I have him on his back and I'm tucked into his side. Head on his shoulder, arm across his waist, thigh over his. "No. He isn't worth it."

We lay there for a bit. Eventually, Tucker's muscles relax and he starts rubbing his thumb on my hip where his hand rests. My shirt rode up when I was trying to get away, leaving me covered in only my panties from the waist down.

We could leave it there. I could tell him about the second helmet another time. But I pull up said big girl panties, and give him what he asked for.

"The other one is like you. He came into the shop. I drugged him and brought him here. First, he hit on Brittany. I mean, who wouldn't? I watched many a man, and women, get sucked into that persona she has perfected with her hair and contouring and boobs always ready to pop out of her top. And who the fuck wears heels all day at work when they don't have to? But she blew him off and he came over to my side of the café."

Tucker's chest jumps under my head as he grunts. I take it as an agreement on the stupid shoes.

"It was pretty much the same. Gave him the rules. Made sure he had his needs met. He opened the cuffs, I was using actual handcuffs and not a lock, with a pocket clip he took off a pen I forgot on the desk. Escaped. Left his helmet behind."

I can feel him thinking. After telling him about the first of my collection, I'm sure he is thinking that there is more to the story than that. There is, but he doesn't need to know it. If he reacted the way he did to me being cheated on...

He isn't going to take that as all of it. "I don't want to accuse you of lying, but there is more than that I'm sure. Omission in this instance is lying though."

Fuck. Fuck, fuck, fuckity fuck.

"He was here for three days. Told me he loved me. Said he understood why I did it. Hell, I didn't understand why I did. I don't know why I took you. Something in me looked at you and said MINE. With him, it was maybe revenge for what happened the first time. Hot guy, hot girl, me being the second choice."

Is that it? Is that why I did it? Well, hooray for me. Glad I figured that out. In both cases.

"You're not going to tell me his name either, are you?" The words rumble under my ear.

Shaking my head, I tilt my chin up to see if he is looking at me and those eyes, shining in what little light manages to get in around the curtains, stare back.

"On the first day, we had sex. I was explaining things to him. Getting him to sign the NDA and stuff you did. When he just kind of jumped me." At Tucker stiffening under me, I rushed on. "Not like that. One minute we were talking, he was signing his papers, and then his lips were on mine and hands and clothes were everywhere."

"We spent that weekend fucking. I didn't put the pen away after he signed, he got it and got out when I went in to work. Left."

"Ruby." That tone tells me he isn't falling for this version either.

"Fucking fine. He promised me forever. Spun tales of our future together. All the jazz that filled my head with what I wanted to hear. He took more than just his bike when he left. He got into my desk. Took a check and wrote it out for fifty grand. Also took copies of my works in progress on a flash drive and published it under his own name. This was before I had even started putting it out there. When I confronted him about the theft, he went to the cops. But I'm not stupid and neither is my attorney. We had screenshots of him bragging on his socials about his wild weekend. A lot. He was smart enough to not name names, but the cops said that with that evidence and the signed contract, it looked like it was mutual. They added in his theft as motive for the claim, trying to flip the script. I never would have slept with him unless he initiated, like you. It could have all just been him tied up until he escaped, like you."

Tucker sits up on his side of the bed, hands wrapped around my bicep as I look up at him pulling me up to my knees so he can look at him face to face. "Names."

With a sad smile, I shake my head. "No. The first gets to live out his days with a nasty scar on his forehead. Got a divorce when she cheated with her golf partner's husband. I got my work back and am now publishing it myself. And then I got the money back, plus some. "

Pushing my hair behind my ear, he pulls me into his lap, my legs on either side of his hips. We're so close to the edge of the bed, I dangle one leg off, toes curling into the plush carpeting. "You said something told you I was yours. Did you mean it? Do you feel something different for me than you did for them?"

I return the hair touching, brushing his off his forehead only for it to fall right back down. Seems tonight is for revelations. I gave him the key to his freedom. He had the chance to leave and instead, he crawled into my bed. Asked me to tell him about parts of my past I'm not happy to talk about. Both moments had me being played for the fool.

Letting him go is going to rip me to pieces I'm not sure I can put back together. But that key was a metaphor. Because it also belonged to my heart. Cheesy and a bit depressing, but the truth. So here I sit. Waiting to see if my past will repeat itself. Throwing it all on the table, all chips in, I answer him. "I meant it. Mine."

I'D DO IT ALL AGAIN

Tucker

Wrapping my arms around her, I twist, flipping her under me. A surprised squeak accompanies the wide eyes looking up from the halo of hair around her head. Elbows planted above her shoulders, I rub my nose on hers before sipping gently from her lips.

Tender is what this moment calls for, but I don't know if I can. For her, I will try anything. Pulling off our clothes, seams popping as I strip us both bare, tossing them into the dark next around the bed. Bracing on one arm, I cup her face, tilting her chin up, kissing along her jaw. Thumb guiding her face to the side, I nip on her thundering pulse before licking over it.

Sighs whisper from her parted lips as my fingers trail down her collar bones. Down the center of her chest. Plumping her breast in my hand, I suck a nipple into my mouth. Humming when she arches off the bed with a sharp gasp when I sink my teeth into the rosy hued flesh. I pay equal attention to the other before sliding down, nipping, licking, kissing silky flesh.

Small red marks mar the pale perfection. Dipping my tongue into her belly button, I nip the upper rim, earning another gasp. Hips twisting and digging into the mattress meet me when I'm low enough to suck in the scent of arousal. Pressing my lips to first one hip bone and then the other, I wedge myself between creamy thighs. Wrapping my arms over her thighs, I anchor my hands in the dips of her hips made just for me to hold her where I want her.

Glistening lips spread when I part her farther. Burrowing my nose in all that wet warmth, I breathe deep. No build up, I latch on to her clit, sucking hard before lathing it with my tongue when her hand slaps on my head before burying her fingers in my hair. Groaning, I follow her hips as she tries to twist away, her hand pushes my head deeper.

Rising enough to see her head thrown back into the twisted bedding we left, I nip at those hips that don't stop moving. Moans and gasps urge me on. Not one panting breath leaving her lips isn't music to my ears. A soundtrack I want to play on repeat for the rest of my life.

Sliding my hands from her hips back around her thighs, I grip her ass and squeeze. Fingerprints will paint her skin, reminding her who she belongs to. Hands pushing her legs wider, I use my thumbs to hold flesh open.

Still hips have me looking up. Ruby is raised on one elbow, watching me while plucking at her hard nipple with the other. Twisting and pinching it into a deep berry color. Maintaining eye contact, I spit on her pussy. With a jerk, she pauses, nipple pulled and pinched from her body, suspended. I do it again.

Air sucked between lips that then breathed out my name, "Tuck."

Shortened to allow for the gasp that follows as I lick her from ass to clit before sliding two fingers in. A pulsing grip grabs them, drawing them deeper into her hot wet pussy. Hand palm up, I rub that soft spot that has her cursing. Hips return to undulating and dancing for me as she collapses back down. Fisting the bedding at her sides.

Popping off her clit, I watch as she moves. Riding my hand. Pressing with my thumb into that pearl of swollen flesh, I enjoy the show of the emotions of her fast approaching orgasm play on her face.

"TUCK!" Voice cracking as she shouts, body clamping on my fingers. I push her through this first one.

"Such a good girl." I look down at where I'm drawing my fingers from her, covered in cum. Sucking my fingers into my mouth, I don't let a drop go to waste. "All this cream for me. But we aren't done."

Shudders rack her chest, head shaking no.

"Aww, you can give me one more. Please, beautiful. Let me feel you cumming on my cock. Let me fill you up. Making us both feel so good."

I don't give her a second to answer. Planting a hand back above her shoulder on the bed, I lift her thigh with the other, notching it on my hip. My dick knows the job he needs doing as he slides in the liquid heat waiting for him. Pushing, he slides home.

Sinking deep, I bump bottom. Ruby's other leg raises from the mattress to grip my hip as I set my hands to hold me up, to watch as I wreck us both. She wraps those long fingers around my wrists and moves with me.

Slowly, I pull back before powering into her, driving a gasp from her. Those blue eyes, pale in the meager light the moon is allowing us, hold mine. Snagging my soul for her to keep.

"Fuck. I can't... I need..." Words fail her as I pick up my pace. She meets me, dancing those hips into mine.

I know she is close when a whine starts filtering into her moans.

"Just a little more. Keep your eyes on me. Let me watch." Eyes open where they drifted closed.

A scream is my answer. Head back, eyes not able to follow my request close, body arching. She is spectacular. The clutching of her pussy milks me into following her. Growling into her neck, I try to keep some of my weight off her as I collapse, twitching.

Still half hard, I pull from her, earning me a pouting whine. Turning to my back, I settle Ruby against my side. Just as she drifts off, she whispers so low I almost don't hear it, "can I keep you."

"Forever." She doesn't hear me as sleep takes her under.

Soft breath blows over my chest as Ruby sleeps on me. I need to let her know that I'm not going anywhere. That I'm in. My mind drifts back to the helmets and the thoughts that had bombarded me that she needs her own. We sell gear at the shop. Not a lot but we have helmets.

Easing from her arms, I stuff a pillow into the space I leave. My suit is draped over the back of her desk chair. Pulling it on feels strange. Like when I get it out in the spring after a winter of not riding. One of the setbacks of living in a northern state.

I move back through Ruby's room, opening the door just enough to slip out. Down the stairs, I pause at a hole in the drywall. In the kitchen I find my boots on a long rug with her shoes. Taking a guess, I open a door and find a dark garage. Feeling for a switch, I flick it on.

Sitting in the middle of the space is my bike. Keys dangle from the ignition. Another switch next to the big door allows me to trigger the motor to raise it. Straddling my bike, I roll it forward before starting it. Engine purring, I smile as I ride into the night to get Ruby a helmet.

Ruby

I don't know what wakes me, only that I am alone when I do. The side of the bed next to me is still warm but cooling rapidly. I don't need to search the room or the house to know Tucker isn't here. I can feel it. The space he occupied echoes with his absence.

Sitting up, the sheet slips down my naked body, making me shiver with its drag on my skin as I listen. In the distance, buried under the sound of my house as it slumbers, the sound of an engine fades. Tears slip silent down my cheeks, dripping on the fabric pooled at my waist before turning into wracking sobs.

Flinging the bedding back, I stand on wobbling knees. I have to take a moment to make sure they will support me. Shoving the tracks off my cheeks with my palms, feet slapping on the cold tiles of the bathroom, I catch myself on the doorframe. Stumbling into the office, using the furniture to help keep me from falling into a heap on the carpet, treading over Tucker's abandoned bed. I push the curtains aside just as the last glow of red taillights disappear.

My breath fogs the glass as I struggle to draw deep enough breaths as my chest heaves with the pain I'm experiencing. Heart rent newly under this cleaving of the poorly bound pieces from past betrayal. Gaze swimming, I toss my head back and scream until my voice gives. All that rage and agony pours from me into the space he left behind.

I was wrong and right. He was mine. Just not forever.

Collapsing into the blankets under my feet, burying my fists in them, I swear I can feel the warmth of Tucker still in them. Smell him embedded in the fabric as if he was what I was clinging to. Crying into soft surfaces as hard as I am leaves little air. Head swimming, I roll to my back.

From the corner of my eye, the saint andrew's mocks me. Throws my trust back in my face. He asked for it and like my heart, ran right over it as he drove away.

I launch myself up and into the hall. I packed all my tools into the dumbwaiter, never sending them back down. Grabbing the ten pound sledgehammer I brought up just in case, I return to the room I can barely stand to be in. Drawing back, I swing with all I have at the wooden structure.

Wood splinters, books tumble, collectables and crystals rain to the floor. I don't stop. Not when my arms can no longer lift the hammer. Not when my body threatens collapse. Fueled with this chapter, this last story, this failed happy ever after, I remove every memory of last night.

I should have known that men don't stay. Even ones that

***

Laying my book down on the arm of the couch to mark my page, I wipe the wet tracks from my cheeks. The watermarks on the pages add to the tale as much as the words written. My emotions splashed across the paper with the grief of the female main character.

Damn it.

WALKING CONTENT WARNING

I love it when an author hits me in the feels. When you can feel as if you are right there, the one experiencing that sadness, that trauma, pulling you to your own knees, that is a well written story.

The kitchen door closing and boots on the hardwood tell me I'm no longer alone. Someone is here to witness my mental break for a fictional moment.

"Another one?" Tears, he has held me as I bawl for someone who doesn't exist. Laughter, looked at me like I had a screw loose as I kicked my feet at whatever moment I just read. Anger, picked up the book I tossed across the room, straightening any damage to return it to me only for me to pick another emotion with the turn of a page. Horniness, acting out all those scenes and reaping the benefit as written smut makes me wet and achy. He has seen them all when I read.

Smiling as I wipe my nose on the cuff of my hoodie, I nod as I look him over. Riding gear so tight it looks painted on covers him from jaw to toes. His helmet is already on and mine is under his arm. "Are we going somewhere?"

Flicking up his visor, I don't have to see his face to know he is smiling. "Thought maybe you might want to get out for a bit.

Maybe get a coffee, a new book since you are almost done with that one. A leaf fell yesterday so pumpkin spice is back."

Tapping a finger on my chin, I pretend to think about it. "Well, I do have to get my daily word count in."

He knows the way to my heart when he says, "we can visit your books in the wild if you want."

Laughing at his choice of words, I jump up, kissing the part that protects his chin, I dart to get dressed for a ride in the fall air.

"Not the red." His voice calls to me where I stand in the mud room in front of our gear closet.

I pause with my hand on that exact outfit, "why not?"

Filling the doorway behind me, he shakes his head. "In that one you're a walking content warning. Those curves shouting ride me. And I want to be able to pay attention, not be distracted by your ass."

Hanger ringing where I pulled the suit off a twinkly tune, I slipped my leg into one side of the one piece suit, hopping around to keep from falling over as I shimmied my way in. Shooting him a wicked grin when I stand with the leather pulled up to my waist. "Red it is then."

Wrapped around the love of my life as we ride down autumn dressed roads, I sigh as we head into town. Leaves dance in our wake as I lean with him in the curves. Tapping the go faster cue when a straight is coming up.

Stop signs are a suggestion when the path is clear. Grind It And Read comes up on our right. I had sat there last week, signing my last book in front of a standing room only crowd with a line down the block.

When presented with a helmet with numbered ping pong balls, I thought I was drawing for a prize. Nope. It was a chapter for a reading. And my luck was laughing when I pulled a spicy one. I am proud to say I was a shade less than fire engine red as I did so to cheers and whistles as my characters got down and dirty. With a projection of each frame behind me. On a screen I thought was just a backdrop. When I say that my hometown is proud of me and my seven weeks at the New York Times' best selling list, that doesn't encompass the love I've gotten.

And next to me the whole time was this man.

The one who rode into my life with a black bike, boots, and attitude.

Review

STARTED

FINISHED

OVERALL ☆☆☆☆☆

SPICE 🌶🌶🌶🌶🌶

WRITING ✒✒✒✒✒

CHARACTERS 👤👤👤👤👤

ENDING ♡♡♡♡♡
*EVEN IF A CLIFFHANGER

NOTES, PAGES, REVIEW

ABOUT
S.L. SIMMONS

The wilds of Appalachia are not big enough to contain the mind that is S.L. Simmons. Instead, she dreams up places where her characters can live out their own happily ever afters because she is living hers.

If you want to know the story of how she and her husband came to be together, feel free to ask. It reads like a missed chance/lost love/reunited trope that will have you saying, 'that would make a good book'. Yes, she is married to a real life *guy from the book*.

It all started with a song that would not leave her alone resulting in a story writing itself in her head before ever seeing the light of day. The voices have multiplied and so have the books. Don't be quick to pigeonhole her into a genre or trope though. She has several works in progress that differ from her breakout series of Mistletoe Fails. Contemporary holiday to paranormal to alien peen, she has a whole brain of stories to tell.

With an OCD and ADD brain fueled by caramel mochaccinos, the space around her protected by a pack of doggos, she writes out the stories that pop into her head at random times.

The best way to keep up with S.L. Simmons is on her website
www.slsimmonswordsmith.com

Blog, calendar of events, merchandise; all there and more.

www.ingramcontent.com/pod-product-compliance
Lightning Source LLC
Chambersburg PA
CBHW011442170626
46807CB00009B/3279